"Just what ... doing to me?"

Frank growled at Beth. Then he pulled her up against his chest, tilted her trembling chin up with one massive finger and kissed her.

It was meant to be another punishment, Beth told herself as she closed her eyes and crossed her fingers. His lips came down on hers and ground away, but only for a second. In that instant of contact, the fierceness shifted to passion.

Fire engulfed her; she shook, sustained only by the strength of his arms. And then he broke it off, pushed her slightly away, and repeated in a querulous, noncomprehending voice, "Just what the hell are you doing to me?"

"Me?" It was hard not to squeak.

"Yes, you," he roared. "Why couldn't it have been your sister?"

Emma Goldrick describes herself as a grandmother first and an author second. She was born and raised in Puerto Rico, where she met her husband, a career military man from Massachusetts. His postings took them all over the world, which often led to mishaps—such as the Christmas they arrived in Germany before their furniture. Emma uses the places she's been as backgrounds for her books, but just in case she runs short of settings, this prolific author and her husband are always making new travel plans.

Books by Emma Goldrick

HARLEQUIN ROMANCE

2661—THE ROAD
2739—THE TROUBLE WITH BRIDGES
2846—TEMPERED BY FIRE
2858—KING OF THE HILL
2889—TEMPORARY PARAGON
2943—TO TAME A TYCOON
2967—THE LATIMORE BRIDE
2984—PILGRIM'S PROMISE
3111—THE GIRL HE LEFT BEHIND

HARLEQUIN PRESENTS

953—HIDDEN TREASURES
1035—IF LOVE BE BLIND
1087—MY BROTHER'S KEEPER
1208—MADELEINE'S MARRIAGE
1281—A HEART AS BIG AS TEXAS
1360—LOVE IS IN THE CARDS

Don't miss any of our special offers. Write to us at the following address for information on our newest releases.

Harlequin Reader Service
P.O. Box 1397, Buffalo, NY 14240
Canadian address: P.O. Box 603,
Fort Erie, Ont. L2A 5X3

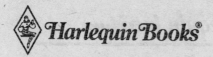
Harlequin Books®

GREAT NEWS...

HARLEQUIN UNVEILS NEW SHIPPING PLANS

For the convenience of customers, Harlequin has announced that Harlequin romances will now be available in stores at these convenient times each month*:

Harlequin Presents, American Romance, Historical, Intrigue:

> May titles: April 10
> June titles: May 8
> July titles: June 5
> August titles: July 10

Harlequin Romance, Superromance, Temptation, Regency Romance:

> May titles: April 24
> June titles: May 22
> July titles: June 19
> August titles: July 24

We hope this new schedule is convenient for you.

With only two trips each month to your local bookseller, you'll never miss any of your favorite authors!

*Please note: There may be slight variations in on-sale dates in your area due to differences in shipping and handling.

*Applicable to U.S. only.

HDATES-RR

Harlequin Intrigue®

Trust No One...

When you are outwitting a cunning killer, confronting dark secrets or unmasking a devious imposter, it's hard to know whom to trust. Strong arms reach out to embrace you—but are they a safe harbor... or a tiger's den?

When you're on the run, do you dare to fall in love?

For heart-stopping suspense and heart-stirring romance, read Harlequin Intrigue. Two new titles each month.

HARLEQUIN INTRIGUE—where you can expect the unexpected.

INTRIGUE

Take 4 bestselling love stories FREE

Plus get a FREE surprise gift!

MISSISSIPPI MISS
Emma Goldrick

𝓗𝓪𝓻𝓵𝓮𝓺𝓾𝓲𝓷 𝓑𝓸𝓸𝓴𝓼

TORONTO • NEW YORK • LONDON
AMSTERDAM • PARIS • SYDNEY • HAMBURG
STOCKHOLM • ATHENS • TOKYO • MILAN

Original hardcover edition published in 1990
by Mills & Boon Limited

ISBN 0-373-03134-3

Harlequin Romance first edition July 1991

To Beth and Joe Wyndham,
who allowed us to share a part of their lives
and their hometown

MISSISSIPPI MISS

CHAPTER ONE

'AND what's more,' Beth Hendley yelled so loudly that her voice squeaked, 'if you don't leave my dog alone I'll bash you with this shovel! Y'hear?'

'I should think everyone in Picayune could hear. Or anyone in Mississippi!' Frank Wylie was at a considerable disadvantage. He had a clipped Yankee accent rather than a deep Southern drawl, he was stuck in the narrow hole at the base of the eight-foot-high hedge that separated his new home from hers, and, after four days of trying, he had almost trapped the mangy mutt which had been digging up his garden. Just another arm's length, that was all he had required. But when he'd squeezed into the hole in the hedge he'd come face-to-shoe with this shovel-armed Joan of Arc!

'Not only a smart aleck, but a Yankee to boot!' There was enough sarcasm in her voice to have won the battle at Shiloh. It had been a hard day at school for Beth, and the autumn term only two weeks along. The old cliché, 'Thank God it's Friday', had rumbled through her head more than once since lunchtime. She needed *something* to bash, and when Fang had come hurtling through the hedge, whimpering, this man's head had seemed to be the ideal target. She hefted her shovel suggestively, straining the elderly red halter-top she wore, and putting more emphasis than necessary on her tatty white shorts. Almost white, that was.

'All right, all right,' Frank grumbled as he lay there, looking up at her. It wasn't a bad view at all. The girl was casually dressed in what might have been hand-me-

7

downs. Her curly black hair came down to her shoulders, where it swung with her every movement. Her soft, rounded face was not exactly beautiful—on the other hand, she was obviously not wearing a bra, and the movements that swayed her hair were also producing some interesting effects on the rest of her well-endowed figure. 'Look, I'll come around the hedge and we'll talk about your mutt—your dog!' That last addition was made as fury chased across the girl's face. How old? Twenty-five, he thought. Thirty. Or maybe even older? A little diplomacy might not go amiss.

'If you come on my property, it's posted,' she said primly as she lowered the shovel and glared at him.

'What's that mean?'

'If my dog bites you on my property after you've been warned, it's not my fault!'

'Hey, great,' he muttered as he tried to wriggle backwards, without avail. 'Southern hospitality?'

'Your sweater is caught on a branch,' Beth commented, obviously pleased by the idea, and unwilling to help.

Frank took a deep breath. 'Bad-tempered' was a statement that had followed him most of his thirty-six years; he had firmly committed himself to creating a different impression in this new career. But it was hard not to take a shot or two. 'I'm glad that I'm giving you so much pleasure. You wouldn't care just to go away for a time?'

'I don't believe I would.' A soft Mississippi contralto, he noted, with just a trace of Cajun in the background. And why not? Picayune was almost at the Louisiana border, and New Orleans was barely an hour away by car. Frank gritted his teeth and shut her out of his mind as he rolled slightly, found the branch that trapped him, and managed to get free. But a closely intertwined privet hedge, carefully trimmed into a barrier, offered more than one trap. Ten minutes later he managed to wriggle free.

He could still hear the woman on the other side of the hedge, comforting her dog, standing in the shade of the tall old oak tree that leaned benignly over her house. What have I let myself in for? he asked himself. Third Avenue is a lovely street, with tree-shaded houses and joined lawns. So I lease the only house separated from its neighbour by a hedge? A hedge that takes years to grow, mind you. This is definitely a spite-hedge! Get over there, Frank-boy, and try a little soft soap!

Committed, he brushed down his baggy trousers, reset his sweater, and managed to find a smile to fit on to his rugged face. Her back was to him as he walked around the edge of the barrier. Bent over, lecturing the tiny mutt that had caused all the trouble, she presented a very delightful view. It took more than a little effort to suppress the desire to pat the target. Gently, of course.

'Miss?'

She whirled around and gasped. He hadn't looked *quite* that big as he'd lain there on his stomach. Nor quite that dangerous. The smile he was wearing was obviously artificial. Behind it she could sense he was grinding his teeth. Beth was not the type of woman to run scared. In fact, in her classroom at Picayune Memorial High School she was known—by a certain number of students—as Hard-hearted Hendley. Nevertheless, this one towered over her five feet four inches, towered enough to make her take a step or two backwards.

'Fang!' Her border collie, the runt of the litter, was backing faster than she. Attempting to set her dog on *this* man was about as useful as trying to bail out the Pearl River with a colander. Fang evidently thought so too. Given a small breathing-space, he turned and ran around to the back of the garage, from which point he settled down to bark his foolish head off.

'Fang?' He was really laughing now, which did nothing to cool Beth's volatile temper.

'You needn't laugh. When I got him I thought he might grow much larger.'

'Ah. A case of misplaced judgement?'

'If you mean to suggest I suffer from a large number of misplaced judgements, then we haven't anything else to say, have we?' As her anger grew she became more stiff, more formal. Even the wind seemed warned off; it stopped toying with her curls, which promptly collapsed against her neck.

'Me? Insult the flower of Southern womanhood?' He kept moving in her direction; she kept backing up until she bumped into the half-opened garage door. Her lungs ached. It had been a long time since she had taken a breath. Breathe, she commanded herself. Breathe, you idiot! A touch of oxygen made its way down into her lungs. She tried three or four more inhalations. His eyes seemed to be glued on something somewhat below her chin. She had no need to look. She knew her breasts were far too big for her tiny frame, and the fact that now *he* knew irritated her no end. Her face turned a violent red, and her temper rose to match.

'Carpetbagger!' she spat.

He had good ears. And fine teeth. They were all on display as he laughed at her. 'I thought the Civil War was long gone. Am I wrong?'

'If you mean the War Between the States, yes.' Why am I so concerned about what *he* thinks? she asked herself frantically. Ships that pass in the night, and all that. Maybe he's only renting? And even if he isn't, why should it bother me?

'But you remember it all?'

'Why not? I teach history.'

'Ah!'

'What's that mean?'

'It means—well—ah! Now about your dog. It *is* your dog, is it not?'

Fang's uproar from his safe hiding-place behind the garage was enough of a din to fetch a police car. Since she had accumulated six complaints in the past three weeks about noisy dogs in a residential area, Beth knew she could hardly afford another. Maybe if I soft-soap him?

'Why, yes, Fang is my dog. Surely you're not afraid of a little dog like that?' All accompanied by an up-and-down search with her big brown eyes, adding a body-language comment of 'a big strong man like you!' A flutter of her long, curly eyelashes fixed the exclamation mark in place.

'Overdoing it a little,' he said, chuckling. 'No, I'm not afraid of your dog, but my roses are.'

'Your roses?'

'My roses. I leased the house next door because of the roses. Fine, beautiful roses, they are. And your dog has come over twice a day to dig at their roots. You'd think there was a body buried there, or something.'

'Maybe there is,' she snapped. 'I'd believe almost anything about the Hurleys! My father hated them, my stepfather hated them—and I——'

'Well, the Hurleys are gone,' he interrupted. 'Now it's the Wylies you have to deal with.' He put out his massive hand in her direction. 'Francis Wylie. My friends call me Frank.'

'How do you do, Mr Wylie?'

His eyebrows arched, and he chuckled again as her very tiny hand gradually moved in his direction, to be swallowed up and gently treasured. 'And...?'

'And? Oh—Hendley. Beth Hendley.' The treasuring continued, beyond need, she told herself, but a gentle tug failed to gain release, and for some insane reason she really didn't *want* to be free of him. There was a certain current of attraction that seemed to flow between them, across the bridge of hands. It was altogether— nice. Beth took a couple of stabilising breaths. 'Francis,' she acknowledged. 'Er—Frank. We heard that someone was moving in next door, but I——'

'Haven't time for gossip, I suppose,' he returned. His other hand came out and joined the first, making a package to contain hers. It's been a long time, he told himself, since I've had a girl of my own. And right next door, too. A lovely, tiny, bad-tempered girl! Just my style. And if I don't stop standing and staring, the sky will fall, Chicken Little!

'Luckily we have a dog to bring us together,' he suggested.

'Oh. Your roses. I'll—speak to Fang about it. I'll——'

'Reason with him?'

'The very word.' It was impossible not to giggle. It's been a long time since I've had a man of my very own, she thought. And at that lovely moment her stepsister Sukey came rattling out of the front door of the house and spoiled everything.

'Beth, can't you stop that mutt of yours from barking? There'll be more complaints, and—well, who have we here?'

It was obvious to Beth that her sister had already seen 'who we have here' through the windows. Sue-Ann was dressed in a swishy shirtwaister whose cerulean sparkle was a match for her carefully coiffed blonde curls, her tall, lithe figure, and her air of sophistication. 'Aren't you going to introduce us, Beth?'

Well, it was too much to expect, Beth told herself glumly. The dumpy brunette and the golden blonde, Act Three. Or was it Act Four? She could hardly remember all those nice young men she had brought home, only to lose them to her sister's charm. But there were other memories too. Of a little blonde child who had lived balanced on a knife-edge, ready to fall off at the slightest opposition. A little ten-year-old girl who had run out to the garage for her bicycle one morning, only to find her father sitting in the front seat of his car, with the motor running, a classic case of suicide. Sue-Ann Foster, who had grown to brittle beauty, and needed to be handled with care and affection. 'Sukey—er—Sue-Ann, this is our new next-door neighbour, Mr Wylie.'

'Mr Wylie,' Sue-Ann acknowledged as she came down on to the grass and offered him a smile, her hand, and her starry blue eyes, perhaps not exactly in that order. Beth tuned out the conversation. It was hardly worth listening to. The end result was already ordained. Sue-Ann would bat her lovely eyelashes—there—the poor man would fall at her feet, she would amuse herself for a day, a week, a month at the outside, and then chew him up and spit him out.

And you're just jealous, her conscience nagged at her. The only thing wrong with the scenario is that it's Sukey playing the heroine. Now if it were Beth Hendley—well! A hand shook her shoulder. 'What?'

'Day-dreaming again! You'll have to excuse Beth, Mr Wylie—Frank. She's the little romantic type. Can't seem to keep her mind on one subject for more than a minute. Beth, Mr Wylie——'

'Can't seem to understand the pair of you,' he interrupted. 'You're sisters, you look entirely different from each other, and her last name is Foster!'

'Half-sisters,' Beth stammered. 'Or maybe not even that close. My mother married her father.'

'But you live amiably together as sisters should,' he drawled. 'That's nice.' There was an altogether gentle sparkle in his eyes. Beth made a note of it, to be filed away under the title of Attractive Nuisances. Dangerously Attractive Nuisances.

'Quite a mix-up,' Sue-Ann said, giggling. 'Her mother left her the house and my father left me all the money.'

'So. Beth teaches school, and you...?'

'Oh, I do social work, committees, things like that,' Sue-Ann responded. 'Even in a small town like Picayune there's always so much that needs doing, you know. Tell me about yourself, Mr Wylie.' She took his arm and guided him around the massive roots of the oak tree, back up the stairs and on to the wide porch, where a white canvas porch-swing awaited them.

'And that's that,' Beth muttered as Fang came quietly back around the garage and sat down beside her. The dog growled, took a half-step towards the porch, then reconsidered. Whatever Fang wanted on the other side of that hedge was still there, while the guardian giant of a man was obviously occupied. Quietly, very quietly, the dog turned around and slouched off for the hole in the hedge.

Saturday morning was a busy time for Beth. She was up just after dawn to take Fang for his regular walk. Up tree-lined Juniper to Goodyear Boulevard, down the boulevard to Forest Street, back to Third, and home. There was a Persian cat that lived on Juniper which Fang hated most desperately. And a pair of dogs that hung out on the corner of Holly seemed not to know their place in the neighbourhood pecking-order. And the rather rotund young man on Forest who was always on guard lest some animal do its duty on his lawn. Altogether a satisfying walk for Fang, who bared his teeth at all his victims, and arrived back home with his tongue hanging out, completely happy with his world.

'You didn't make my breakfast,' Sue-Ann complained as Beth and the dog rambled into the kitchen.

'I didn't think you wanted it,' Beth returned. 'You were out until all hours of the night. I thought you'd sleep in.'

'Well, I didn't,' her sister complained. 'Things didn't quite work out. But you can——'

'No, I'm afraid I can't,' Beth interrupted. 'I have a tutoring group at the school this morning. Some of the boys on the football team are having a problem, and I offered to coach them.'

'You did that last year,' Sue-Ann muttered. 'And the year before. Surely your sister comes before a bunch of overgrown high-school kids?'

'I wish they were,' Beth said, sighing. 'Overgrown, I mean. We could use a couple of two-hundred-and-twenty-pound players this year. Look after Fang for me?'

'I don't have the time.'

No, nothing ever changes, Beth thought as she tugged the reluctant dog behind her out into the back yard and fastened him to his long chain. She had been twenty-one when the girls had lost Beth's mother. Sue-Ann had been only thirteen. And now, seven years later, they were still living together in an uneasy peace. All the responsibilities seemed inevitably to fall on Beth's shoulders, all the fun on Sue-Ann's. But you wouldn't have it any other way, she told herself. Your sister will find out who she is one of these days, and you'll be relieved of the

tender burden that mother placed on you. Maybe she'll
get married. Maybe she'll marry Mr Wylie and they'll
live next door and have four kids and I'll be a busy aunt
and—lord, why does it hurt so much to think of that?
Is it the 'marriage' part or the 'Mr Wylie' part?

Disgusted with herself, Beth packed her book-bag and
headed back to the boulevard and the high school. Life
was too complicated. She loved her crazy, mixed-up
sister; had always *wanted* a sister to love; considered Sue-
Ann her Christian duty. But there were times when Sukey
was a little—difficult. And so Beth strode off on her
usual walk to work. Over to Goodyear, the six-lane
avenue, tree-lined, with a divider in the middle, up past
the Crosby Memorial Library to the high school. Crosby
Memorial Hospital stood across the street. The huge
white pillars of the Baptist church were close by, and
the more prosaic city hall stood on the corner. Crosby
was a name to be reckoned with in Picayune. Crosby
and Thigpen.

Five young men were waiting for her on the front steps,
but the sunshine was too good to waste. She led them
around to the lawn that separated school from library,
and set them to work. 'Larry,' she asked after a quick
head-count, 'Billy Joe isn't coming?'

The tall, gangly football player shrugged his shoulders.
'Ain't nobody can tell what Billy Joe's goin' to do,' he
reported.

Beth shook her head. Billy Joe was undoubtedly
planning to be the major problem of the football season.
There was always one, but the worst tack she could take
would be to call attention to the fact. 'Yes, well, Larry,'
she chuckled. 'There ain't no such word as ain't.'

'My dad's a Beat supervisor,' he replied, 'and he says
ain't all the time.'

'Yes, but he doesn't have to take the English test next Tuesday,' she teased. And then, because there had been a game the night before, she shushed the laughter and set to work with them individually.

By eleven o'clock she felt they had done as much as could be expected. As her own father, a long-dead army officer, had always said, 'The mind can accept only as much as the seat can endure.' Which brought her home at eleven-thirty to find Mr Wylie and her sister waiting on the front porch.

'Well,' he said. It wasn't a pleasant 'well'. More like a guillotine 'well', to tell the truth. And her sister was grinning, standing slightly behind his shoulder. It took no magic for Beth to realise she was in trouble, and her sister had something to do with it.

'Yes, well,' she offered tentatively. 'I hope you've had a good morning?'

'I'm sure you do,' he said. 'I suppose you've been off to the swimming-pool? Having a good time? While your dog chewed his way through half my flowers!'

'I—really—not exactly,' she managed. 'And it's not possible that Fang was in your garden. I chained him up myself, and he can't chew his way through a quarter-inch steel chain!' So there, she wanted to add, but hadn't the courage. 'Where is my dog?'

'Locked in the garage,' he told her. 'That dog is mad! And he actually tried to bite me!'

'That's not possible,' Beth replied firmly. 'He couldn't have bitten through the chain, and he couldn't have bitten...' Her words petered out as he set one massive foot up on the porch rail. She could see the tears in the leg of his trousers, and the scratches underneath. It's time to change my attack, Beth told herself.

'So what did you do to aggravate my dog and make him bite you? Those aren't bites, they're scratches.

Climbing through the hedge again, were you?' she snapped. 'Just supposing, for theoretical purposes, that Fang *might* have got into your yard——'

'Theoretical, hell!' he yelled, interrupting. 'Your animal is a threat to life and limb, and——' And that was the moment that Fang, hearing the voice of his mistress, howled.

Beth had no further time for discussion. Her dog was obviously in agony. She whirled around and ran for the garage. The door was fastened shut by an unlocked padlock. She managed to fumble it out, all the while promising her animal that help was coming. As usual, she had trouble raising the overhead door. As the sunlight penetrated the dark interior she found Fang quivering by the left front wheel of Sue-Ann's Porsche. Before the door was completely up she abandoned it and dived for the dog. As soon as her hands were off the door, it began to slide shut again, only to be stopped and forced back by a healthy heave and a few short words.

'Now tell me about how your dog can't get off his chain,' he said, looming ominously over her.

'Tell me how my dog got blood on his head!' she screamed at him.

'The damn fool——'

'Don't you curse my dog.' Beth picked up the little armful and began to cuddle him. Fang accepted the tribute and licked her nose as she stalked by Frank Wylie, out into the sunshine.

'Your dog——'

'I don't want to hear anything more about *my dog* from you, you—you dog-beater! Get off my land! I'm going to report you to the—to the——' For the life of her she couldn't think to whom all these tribulations should be reported. 'To the United Nations!' she yelled at him as she stomped up the stairs, slammed the door behind her, and carried her dog out to the kitchen. His wounds proved to be very tiny indeed. Which did nothing to cover her embarrassment, and thus increased her temper.

About an hour later her sister sidled into the kitchen, a wary look her eyes. 'Is it safe?'

'Yes, it's safe,' Beth said glumly. 'I've done it again, haven't I? I promise myself every day that I won't lose my temper, but that man—Sue-Ann, how do you suppose Fang got off his chain?'

'I'm afraid I'm responsible,' her sister said. 'He was howling, and he got tangled up in the chain, so I went to straighten him out—and he got away from me. I'm really sorry, Beth.'

Beth shook her head slowly from side to side. There was no hope for her sister's reform. Sue-Ann's mind wandered like a butterfly, flitting from goal to goal with neither meanness nor malice. Or so Beth had thought over all those years. 'So that was the way of it? Well, water over the dam. Now I suppose I'll have to apologise to him.'

'You'll have plenty of time,' Sue-Ann announced. 'I invited him to dinner tonight.'

'Oh, my lord. I don't like him that much that I'd want to share salt with him. What stroke of madness led you to do that?'

'He took me out to Le Bois Restaurant last night, Beth. We had a scrumptious dinner. You wouldn't believe. I just *had* to do *something* in return.'

'Le Bois? The one in town, or the one out in Mercer?'

'In town, of course. I don't exactly dig the country atmosphere.'

'No, I guess you don't,' Beth said, sighing. *She* did, and the Le Bois Restaurant out in the woodland in

Mercer was her ideal. But Picayune was distinctly short of bachelors these days, looking to take an *elderly* schoolteacher out for a big evening. She shook her head in disgust. 'A big-time spender?' Beth mused. 'What is he, some super-executive from out at the Space Center?'

'I don't know. That's one of the things I have to find out.'

'So what do you expect to serve him tonight? Fried chicken?'

'Oh, no, Beth, not that. It's got to be something fancy. Beef Wellington, I thought, and——'

'You know you can't cook anything except fried chicken,' Beth commented. 'And I don't think I'd want to share the——'

'That's perfectly all right,' Sue-Ann interrupted eagerly. 'You don't have to come to table with us. That will give you more time, you know.'

'More time for what?' It was one of those questions you wished you had never asked before the last word ran out of your mouth!

'More time for you to cook the dinner.' Sue-Ann was bubbling with good humour now. 'Beef Wellington, fresh asparagus, rice pilaff. And I'm sure you could think up a bunch of other fine dishes! Oh, thank you, Beth. You're the best sister a girl ever had!'

She was out the door, singing at the top of her voice, before Beth managed to close her mouth.

The dinner preparations took the rest of the afternoon. Beth was tired to begin with. She had spent Friday night at the football game, where the Picayune Maroon Tide had swept to a startling victory over the Long Beach team and her squad of cheerleaders had done well with several of their new routines. Then the Saturday morning tutorial sessions, not exactly a piece of cake. So she drove back home after grocery shopping at Delchamps, doing sums in her head. Just the purchase of the ingredients had ruined her food budget for the month.

'Is everything ready?' Sue-Ann danced into the kitchen at six-thirty, twirling to demonstrate her new eau-de-Nil silk dress. There was more to the skirt than there was to the bodice, but Beth was too tired to comment. She waved a hand vaguely towards the stove.

'Everything.'

'And what are you having for supper?'

'A bologna sandwich,' Beth replied. 'But it's your meal, and your clean-up, Sue-Ann.'

'Oh—but you've made such a mess of the kitchen!' Under her sister's glare Sue-Ann recanted. 'But of course I'll do it all up before I go to bed. Whoever had a nicer sister!'

'Whoever indeed,' Beth said, sighing, as her sister danced out of the room, her blonde hair swinging in the breeze off the porch. 'Whoever indeed.' Wearily she pushed her own dark curls off her neck, took one more look through the menu, then, too tired to make herself anything to eat, pushed a space clear on the kitchen table and opened her briefcase.

It was always with her, that briefcase, loaded with papers. The easy way out, in any high school, was to give 'true or false' tests, sophisticated guessing-games. But Beth insisted that she was not only testing history, but writing as well. As a result her every test consisted of essays, every paper had to be read word for word, marks had to be attached, and comments entered. Five classes a day, twenty-eight students per class, five days a week. Her correction time was astronomical.

From time to time Sue-Ann came back into the kitchen to exchange plates, humming a happy tune. 'Going well?' Beth enquired as she stopped to rub her tired neck.

'Lovely,' her sister answered. 'Lovely. The food is almost as delicious as *he* is.'

'Yes, well, don't let him bite you.' Beth lowered her head again and began making wide red slash-marks on the paper in front of her. She was not one to concentrate on battlefields, but there was no way she could ignore the Battle of Lexington being fought in Kentucky rather than in Massachusetts.

At eight o'clock she stopped. The little pendulum clock on the wall struck the hour at the same moment that the kitchen door flew open and banged against its rubber stop. 'So this is where you're hiding.'

'Hiding?' He was big and tall and handsome and angry. She could feel the sparks flying in her direction. He came over and leaned one hip on the kitchen table and glared.

'Hiding,' he affirmed. 'Your sister has gone to all this trouble to make an outstanding dinner, and you—just hide in the kitchen! And I suppose this is your excuse?' He picked up one of the well-decorated papers and glanced over it.

'Excuse?' Beth was too tired to make a scene, but not too tired to be entirely silent. 'No, it's not my excuse, it's my living. I trust you enjoyed the meal?'

'Marvellous. When I first saw your sister I could have sworn she couldn't boil water, but this meal was perfect. I suppose you got your share before it came to the table?'

'Is that an accusation?'

'Accusation? Well, perhaps it is. What is it with you? Were you born with a chip on your shoulder?'

'It may be that I just don't like dictatorial men,' she snapped. 'Now if you wouldn't mind, I'd appreciate your returning to the front of the house.'

'Somebody ought to teach you a lesson.' One of his long arms snatched her up out of her chair without warning. Papers flew helter-skelter. Unable to catch her breath, Beth found herself imprisoned in those strong, warm arms. She hung there momentarily, and then her temper broke through.

'Turn me loose, you—you Mastodon. Turn me loose or I'll——'

'Or you'll what?' Said softly, but totally clear, because his mouth was hardly an inch or two from her ear. She opened her mouth to make a comment, only to find his lips on hers, blocking the words. His lips on hers, his tongue questing through into the softness of her, his arms pressing her hard against his steel chest. Things became very hazy for Beth Hendley. She managed a wriggle or two and then gave it up. Fighting was hardly worth the effort, when she so much enjoyed what was going on!

When he finally put her down she was gasping for breath, barely managing to fight off the impulse-signals running up and down her spine, and the tingling sensation from where her breasts had been flattened against him. She blinked her eyes a couple of times, and managed to bring him into focus.

He looked like a man who had decided to wrestle with a house-cat, only to find out it was a lioness. The pair of them stared at each other, and then he cleared his throat and began brushing at the flour his suit jacket had accumulated from her apron.

'Ooh!' Sue-Ann was at the door, her mouth pursed in a baby-doll protest. Frank Wylie stepped back a couple more paces, then turned on his heel and fled through the door.

'Really, Beth.' Sue-Ann could also cry on command. One demonstration tear was poised to run down her cheek. 'He's mine, Elizabeth Hendley. You know that!'

'I won't argue the point,' Beth returned wearily. 'I didn't have anything to do with that. It was all his idea to punish me. Why don't you go and ask him why he did it?'

Sue-Ann nibbled on her lip as she watched Beth with those huge, glistening blue eyes. 'Well,' she said, and turned to run after Wylie.

'Well, indeed,' Beth whispered to herself as she gently touched her bruised lips. 'He certainly taught *me* a lesson!'

On Monday morning Beth struggled out of bed at six o'clock, feeling the tiredness of virtue. All her papers were graded, all her marks entered into her book, all her lesson plans reviewed. Only her feet gave her a problem. She had taken a very long walk on Sunday. Anything to get her away from the sorrowful looks Sue-Ann was presenting.

Fang met her in the kitchen, jumping up and down madly as he usually did. She fed him, set water in his outside dish, and chained him up on his travelling-leash, the one that allowed him free access to the entire yard.

For her own breakfast Beth managed her usual toast, orange juice and coffee. She peeped in on Sue-Ann. As usual, her sister was blissfully asleep, a huge smile on her face, her blankets scattered half on the floor, her lace-trimmed nightgown askew. It wouldn't be worth trying to awaken her, Beth knew from experience. So instead she scribbled a quick note, straightened a blanket over the recumbent form, and went back to her own room to slip into her teaching uniform.

There was no time required for selection. In the Mississippi heat she kept a collection of light cotton shirtwaisters. In any colour, she charged herself sarcastically, as long as you like navy blue. Her hair was the same—brushed out until it shone down to her shoulders.

It would soon be higher, she knew, as soon as the curls popped back into control after being momentarily brushed out.

She took one extra peep in her mirror. What was *he* doing at this time of day? Getting ready to go out to the Space Center? Why did he kiss me like that? Punishment? For what, dear lord? Her fingers scrubbed at her lips, but the uneasy feeling would just not go away.

'Come on, lady,' she snapped at herself. 'Give it up! He was trying to teach you a lesson!'

With briefcase in hand she stopped by the back yard to say goodbye to Fang. 'And you behave yourself,' she admonished, as the little animal danced around her, tangling her in his chain. 'Behave,' she repeated.

Her unrepentant dog whined. His low, mournful howl followed her as she went around the house and walked off towards the school.

It was a cool morning, with promise of a hot day to follow. A breeze played with the swaying boughs of the trees. Beth breathed deeply. The air was redolent of late flowers. Picayune was a city bustling with activity, but to the twenty thousand people who lived in and around, it was a small country town with growing-pains.

As soon as she moved out of the shaded pavements into the wide open area around the school she could feel the heat penetrating the thin cotton of her dress. There were few people to be seen; most of the students would not arrive for another half-hour, but Beth always came early; she needed the extra time. She marched into her home-room, plumped her briefcase down on the desk, and rested her chin in the palms of her hands. There were so many things to be done—as there were on any school day. She tugged her lesson plans for the day out of her case and began to review them again.

The loudspeaker on the wall grumbled and cleared its throat. 'Miss Hendley?' Repeated three times before it secured her full attention.

'Yes?'

'The new assistant principal wants to know if you are in your room.'

'Yes, I am.' The machine clicked off. Beth toyed with her pencil for a moment. The new assistant principal? She had heard some vague rumours, but since they didn't concern her, she had shrugged them off. And already he was checking up on teachers? Beth looked up at the classroom clock. She was still twenty minutes earlier than required. Shrugging her shoulders, she went back to the lesson plans.

She was totally engrossed in the role-playing mode she had laid on for the senior history class when she vaguely heard the door to her classroom open and close. 'Miss Hendley?' A deep male voice. She looked up. And up.

'Oh, dear lord,' she muttered.

'So it would seem,' Frank Wylie said bleakly.

CHAPTER TWO

'I FOUND this on my desk this morning, Miss Hendley.' Frank Wylie shoved a folded piece of paper in her face. Beth reached for the paper. He snatched it back, carefully unfolded it, and set it flat on the desk in front of her. 'Well?'

'Well, what—sir?' Beth pushed her chair back and stood up. I need all the advantages I can get, she told herself as she tugged her dress into a semblance of order and glared up at him. 'It's a standard form.'

'I know that,' he said disgustedly. 'It's a warning slip. The term is only in its third week today, and you predict that Billy Joe Mowbray is going to flunk history in the first quarter? What are you, some sort of clairvoyant? This *is* your signature, isn't it?'

'Yes!' Over his shoulder she could see the first students filter into the room, but clamping a lid on her temper was almost more than she could do. 'Yes,' she repeated in a whisper. 'Did you think it was a forgery? I'm also a teacher with six years of classroom experience, *Mr* Wylie. Can you say as much?'

He looked over his shoulder, then turned and leaned down to her. 'If Billy Joe flunks he can't play football,' he hissed. 'I'm spending half my time in this school getting students to join extra-curricular activities. And here you're working in just the opposite direction. Billy Joe may not be our best student, but he is a weathervane. Flunk him this first quarter, and he can't play. We don't want that to happen!'

'Oh? *We* don't?'

27

Suddenly he took on the appearance of a man trying to reason with an idiot. He leaned closer, talking softly. 'Listen up, lady. In American school systems team sports like baseball, football, basketball and track have become an integral part of the school function. Students who might not otherwise try to succeed in the classroom work harder at maths when they know an academic failure will drop them out of the sports programme. Or the drama club, or the chess club. Or anything. Participation develops *esprit de corps*, a sense of belonging! So we expect our teachers to do their best to bring all this to the attention of the students. Got it?'

Beth Hendley had already put up with more patronising than she could stand, and was having a great deal of trouble controlling her facial muscles. 'I don't speak French,' she said with a meek sigh, 'and it doesn't seem to be working with Billy Joe.'

'It takes time,' he muttered angrily. 'Time and assistance from the faculty.'

Beth, who knew all this and a great deal more besides, did her best to hide her anger, but it was leaking out the sides of her brilliant eyes. 'How long do you expect to be with us, Mr Wylie?' she asked.

'About a year,' he snapped. 'What does that have to do with anything?'

'Well—that's rather a long time. A whole year. I'm afraid you'll be trying to tell me more than I'd care to know about this subject!'

He managed to heave a sigh. The room was filling rapidly. 'Look,' he spat at her, 'I want you to take this paper back and reconsider the implications.'

'Or?'

'Just *do* it, Miss Hendley. I don't intend to let you take out your bad temper on the students. How in the world did you ever get a teaching job, anyway?'

'Influence,' she snapped, shaking with fury. 'Political influence. Is there anything else, Mr Wylie?'

He looked around the classroom and then back at her. 'Do what you're told,' he ordered gruffly, and walked out the door.

'Do what you're told,' she muttered under her breath. It was unbearable. A little ceramic paperweight stood on the corner of her desk, a souvenir of her trip to Jackson, Mississippi. She picked it up, still fuming as she watched his massive back saunter towards the door. Her hand squeezed the solid little figure until it seemed to become smaller. Throw it at him, her anger said. Don't you dare. Ladies never behave like that. It was the voice of her mother. 'Ladies never behave like that,' Beth muttered.

Her hand trembled with rage. The little ceramic paperweight, advertised as unbreakable, fell to the floor and smashed into a hundred little pieces.

The noise had been enough to calm Beth down. She looked at the paperweight, feeling as stupid as one could be. She could call for a janitor, and there would be questions galore. Or, for a teacher with a considerable temper, she could keep a broom in the cupboard at the rear of the room. Which she did. And two volunteers were already parading the instrument down the aisle between the desks. A large number of her students were giggling.

So Beth shook her head, grinned back at them, and said, 'Do as I say do, not as I do do.' And next Wednesday night at prayer meeting, she told herself morosely, I must ask all the congregation to help me petition for a more placid temper.

Beth blushed and made busy work for herself, leafing through her lesson plan. It was hard to be a hard-boiled teacher when one's core was as mushy as a marshmallow.

*　　*　　*

Out in the hall Frank Wylie paused for a moment. He heard the tinkle of breakage, but hadn't the courage to look back into the school-room. No woman—except his Aunt Harriet—had ever got under his skin so quickly, nor left him so full of guilt. 'Crazy,' he muttered. The tall, thin boy rushing down the corridor, late for class, hesitated as if he had been reprimanded.

'I couldn't help it,' the boy muttered, almost in tears.

'I know you couldn't,' Frank responded, shaking his head dolefully. 'Your dog chewed up your homework papers, right?'

'How did you know?' The boy took one more quick look at the massive man leaning against the wall, and hurried around him into the classroom.

And so much for *that*, Frank Wylie, he told himself. Dr Frank Wylie. Don't you have anything better to do than scare fifteen-year-old kids in the hallways? Or yell at teachers whom you'd rather kiss than kill? Your father never got further than the fourth grade, but he had more smartness in his little finger than you have in your whole body, Frank!

It was not a comfortable musing. He made his way down the corridor, shaking his head. The high school was a confusion; it had once been the junior high school, but when commitments had required more space the two schools had exchanged buildings, and an addition was growing at a rapid pace for additional classrooms and laboratories. There was a muted bustle as he entered the administrative area. The school secretary was sitting at a computer keyboard, a mixed expression on her face as she watched the machine perform. Margaret Lewis, the principal, came out of the inner office at the same moment.

'Well, Frank. An unveiling?'

'So to speak,' he murmured as he tried to cheer the secretary with a smile. 'It doesn't look as if Cora was too sure of its blessings.'

'It's—a little intimidating,' the secretary replied. 'I don't understand half of what's going on!'

'Dr Wylie, as you remember, Cora, has volunteered to serve at our school for a year at his own expense, to implement some of the ideas he expressed in his doctoral thesis. His basic idea was that if you can't keep a student inside the school, and interested, you can't educate him worth a darn.'

'But—but this?' Cora asked, gesturing towards the machine, which was clicking happily away.

'That's the first step,' Frank said, chuckling. 'First we have to make sure that the students *attend*. The computer has in its memory a complete record of each student. When you type up the absentee list each morning, the computer then goes through its file and makes an automatic telephone call to the parents of each student not present. The machine then tapes whatever excuses the parent has to offer, and makes a record of it in the student file. Anybody in the office can monitor that file any time they wish. And when a child comes up absent for more than two days the machine will turn itself on and tell you about it.'

'But the cost,' Cora sighed. 'The school committee will have fits!'

'That's not so,' Margaret contributed. 'Mississippi was once the lowest state in the Union where education is concerned; now, statewide, although we can't spend as much money as some of the richer states, we're being very careful to get every penny's worth out of what we've got, and the statewide college entrance scores prove how effective we've been. Tell her, Frank.'

'There's not much to tell,' he said. 'The computer manufacturer wants his machine tested—for free. The Southern Bell Telephone Company wants to expand the use of its lines, so it's rented them to us at one dollar a year. And so the only drain is on you and your fingers, Cora.'

'Which is a losing cause,' Cora said, flinging up her hands.

'Which is bound to be a winner,' he said, trying to cheer her up. 'By this time next week you'll have it all down pat.'

'I should live so long,' the secretary replied, and then giggled. 'But it *is* fun!'

'Come into the office for a minute, Frank,' the principal invited. He ambled after her, and closed the door behind him. 'You know,' she said, as she settled into her chair, 'I think I've found the perfect partner for the other part of your programme. The one about developing more interesting presentations within the curriculum.'

'Someone with imagination?'

'More than you could ever believe.'

'And who is this paragon?'

'Beth Hendley.'

'Oh, my—Hard-hearted Hendley?' In their short acquaintance Frank knew the value of Margaret Lewis's opinions, but this one brought him up sharply. Am I going to be haunted by this—paragon? he asked himself. I've planned to be here only one year, but that shrew could make it feel like a lifetime!

'The very one.' And then, almost as if it were an afterthought, 'Are you married, Frank?'

What with one thing and another, the busy day proved to be not too unbearable, and when the last bell of the last class had rung Beth Hendley found herself back at her desk, with nothing to handle except the warning report that Dictator Wylie had dropped on her desk. She fingered it carefully. Billy Joe was a transfer student, under dubious conditions. His school papers had come from Hattiesburg, where academically he had scored a passing sixty-five per cent in all his subjects. Which immediately had made Beth suspicious.

He had come to live with his aunt out in Beat Five, a very comfortable neighbourhood indeed. And his sole ambition was to be the paramount football running back in the State of Mississippi. Beth took one more quick look in her mark-book. 'Reconsider,' Wylie had said.

'And so I have,' she said firmly as she pulled another blank warning slip from her desk and filled it out again. And just to make sure, on the way home she detoured by the administrative office and dropped the paper in the principal's 'In' basket. She walked home very jauntily, feeling the strength of righteous conviction— and just the slightest amount of trepidation at having snubbed His High and Mightiness, Mr Frank Wylie.

There were hammering noises from next door as she walked up the drive of her house. And an occasional short four-letter expletive. Mr Wylie was clearly busy at something other than annoying classroom teachers. Erecting a gallows? her conscience teased. Curiosity drove her. She walked over to the hole in the hedge and bent over to peer through. A pair of angry dark eyes met hers. Neighbour Wylie was busy pounding a wire screen into the ground to block the hole.

'You——' he said, and seemed to swallow his tongue. Beth sat back on her heels, tucking her skirts beneath her. It was fascinating to watch a full-grown man turn from tan to ruddy red. She could almost see the steam rising from somewhere around his ears. 'Your damn dog——' he sputtered.

'You shouldn't curse,' she returned mildly. 'I'll pray for you.'

'Do that,' he growled. 'Go away. And take your—dog—with you! You deserve each other!'

It wasn't the words, it was his expression that finally sank in. 'Oh, my,' Beth exclaimed, and ran for the back yard. Fang's chain lay limply in the grass; there was no sign of the dog. Fear sent a little spurt up her spine. She raced for the kitchen door.

'Sue-Ann? Sue-Ann!' Her sister came languidly into the kitchen, one hand holding a wine glass. There was something curious about the girl's sulky expression. 'Fang. What happened to Fang?'

Her sister shrugged her shoulders and sipped at the wine.

'Sue-Ann, this is no laughing matter. What happened?'

'Your dog—got loose, and ran wild next door.'

'I don't like the way you say that. Got loose? How, got loose? Where's Fang?'

'I turned him loose, if you must know.' Sue-Ann looked at her accusingly.

'Turned him loose? Dear lord, why?'

'You know why,' her sister said bitterly. 'He's mine. You had no right to kiss him. I was just paying you back!' There seemed to be no need for discussion about who *he* was.

'I don't believe it,' Beth murmured, aghast. 'I just don't believe it!'

'Believe it.'

Beth strode across the intervening space and reached up to give her sister a good shake. 'You were more adult when you were fifteen, Sukey. Why in the name of all that's holy would you want to get mad at me and take it out on my dog? I've told you more than once that I have no interest in Mr Wylie. Or maybe I do. I'd like to murder him. And maybe you too! Where——?'

'At the dog-pound.' Beth's intensity had finally got through. Tears were forming in the blonde's eyes. Beth gave her one last shake and then ran for the door. Frank Wylie grabbed at her arm as she tried to bypass him on the outside stairs.

'Let go of me,' she muttered, trying to shake loose.

'Not until you look at something,' he returned coldly. 'Not only did you set your dog on me, did you have to beat up on your sister?' Beth whirled around. Sue-Ann was leaning against the front door-jamb, tears streaking her face, innocence personified. Beth's temper broke loose again.

'Yes,' she raged. 'And I'll do the same to you if you don't look out!' She flexed both hands, making claws out of her red-enamelled fingernails.

'Tough luck,' he muttered. 'I'm looking out. And I'm a hell of a lot bigger than you are.'

'You should be so lucky!' But rage in a five-foot-four female could hardly compete with the same feelings in a six-foot-two male. He dragged her off the steps, down to the pavement, and up into his own garden.

'There,' he said roughly, tugging her, almost throwing her up ahead of him. Beth's head was spinning as she fought to maintain her balance. It took more than a moment to recover. At her feet were the remnants of a well-dug flower-bed, with stalks lying in every direction, and a few tatters of some very fine rose buds among the litter.

'Your dog...' he muttered, his face in a fury. 'Your damn dog!'

'Well, you needn't curse,' she retorted.

'I swear to heaven I'll curse if I damn well want to!'
Said at about the level of a well-bred hurricane. Beth
ducked reflexively, and then her defensive temper came
to the rescue.

'And blasphemy as well,' she announced as she folded
her hands primly behind her back. 'I'm sure my dog—
if my dog is responsible—has some good reason
for——'

'Damn your dog!' he roared. 'Somebody buried a dead
cat there. But that's no reason for——' Beth moved a
nervous step or two away from him. His eyes seemed to
have widened, there was a complex look on his face that
seemed to be halfway between murder and apoplexy, and
then he grabbed her shoulders. Not too gently, either.

'For pity's sake,' he growled at her, 'just what the hell
are you doing to me?' And with that he pulled her up
against his chest, tilted her trembling chin up with one
massive finger, and kissed her.

It was meant to be another punishment, Beth told
herself as she closed her eyes and crossed her fingers.
His lips came down on hers and ground away, but only
for a second. In that instant of contact the fierceness
shifted to passion. His grip on her shoulders slackened.
One of his hands moved to caress her back gently in a
teasing, circular movement. Her breasts flattened against
the rigid muscles of his chest. His tongue prodded at her
lips. She opened her mouth without thinking. Fire
engulfed her; she shook, sustained only by the strength
of his arms. And then he broke it off, pushed her slightly
away, and repeated in a querulous, non-comprehending
voice, 'Just what the hell are you doing to me?'

'Me?' It was hard not to squeak. Hard not to blubber.

'Yes, *you*,' he roared. 'Why the hell couldn't it be
your sister?'

'I—I don't know what you're talking about.'

'No, of course you don't,' he muttered as he stared down into her eyes. 'Miss Goody Two-Shoes! My gawd, what did I do to deserve this?'

Beth gathered up her strength and pushed herself away from him, still short of breath. 'I don't know what you're talking about,' she stammered, 'but you undoubtedly deserve it all, and then some—whatever it is. Try coming to prayer meeting, Wednesday night!'

'And that's another thing,' he muttered. He shoved his hands into his pockets, glared at her for a moment longer. 'Hymn-singing Methodists! Lord protect me——'

'Bible-thumping Baptist,' she interjected angrily. 'Southern Baptist. You could use a little hymn-singing, Mr Wylie. And let me tell you something else, if my dog——'

But she was talking to air. He spun on his heels, stomped up into his own house, and slammed the door behind him, leaving Beth teetering on her heels, in full disarray.

Disgusted at the world, she did her best to rearrange herself, muttering all the while. His door had closed behind him like the crack of doom. There seemed to be no hope in that direction. What did he mean? she thought. What does he think I'm doing to him? I was practically minding my own business, and he snatched me up like some vagabond. I wonder if I could charge him with kidnapping? And the cat—the buried cat? He's been maintaining an attractive nuisance under his rose-bed! No wonder Fang kept digging there. A cat? Good lord. Murgatroyd? I thought she had run away six months ago. Those Hurleys! Those double-dealing, two-timing, cat-murdering Hurleys!

Luckily the Hurleys have moved to the end of the world, Huntsville, Alabama, or I would—— Nervously her hand rubbed across her lips. The taste could not be removed. He had branded her as fully as if he had used a hot iron. A thoroughly disreputable man!

There were times when Beth Hendley wished she were *not* a devout Baptist. Four or five words she had heard from the boys' athletic teams came to mind. They might just fit the circumstances, and could easily relieve her temper—but she hadn't the courage to use them. Dejectedly she turned around and walked back down to the pavement, where she came to a dead stop. If he's such a disreputable fellow, Beth Hendley asked herself, why did I enjoy the kissing part so much? She might have wondered until supper, but Fang's predicament gradually filtered back into her mind. She walked slowly up the incline to her garage, backed her Ford Escort out into the street, and went off to do battle with the animal control officer.

'But—Rose,' Beth objected weakly. Rose Marston, the assistant dog officer, stood adamantly on the other side of the counter, her badge glaring in the afternoon sun.

'Look, Beth, there's nothing I can do for you. After all, this is the fourth time we've policed up your animal. You're lucky that the Animal Officer isn't in this afternoon. You know what *he'd* say!'

'I—suppose he's angry?'

'More than that,' Rose replied. 'He went out on patrol specifically so he wouldn't have to talk to you. Said he didn't want to bite your head off, you being his daughter's teacher and all, but he couldn't guarantee that he wouldn't!'

'All right.' Dejected, Beth took a swipe at her leaking eye. 'I *do* get to take Fang home?'

'Yes. Maybe that's one of your problems,' Rose offered. 'He's only a pup. You give him a name like

Fang, he's apt to try to live up to it. You might rename him. Something like Pansy, for example.'

'Oh, lord, Pansy?'

'Well, it was only a suggestion. And you have to appear in Municipal Court on Saturday. Mind you, they've made an exception because you're a teacher, you know. Mr Scruggs has filed a complaint.'

'Mr Scruggs? The chairman of the school committee?' Not my day, Beth told herself morosely. A fight with the assistant principal, a temper completely lost—and in school at that—a kiss from my neighbour, who thinks he has to punish me, and now my dog has—what?

'What did Fang do to Mr Scruggs?' she asked tentatively.

'To him? Nothing. But his Persian cat, wow! That tree is maybe fifty feet high, and the cat went up to the top in Olympic time. Had to call the fire department ladder truck to get him down.'

'And I suppose somebody has to pay the bill,' Beth mourned. 'Pansy? I don't think Fang would like that.'

'Yes, well, we all have problems.' Rose went into the back to bring out the dog. Fang squirmed out of the officer's arms as soon as he saw his mistress, and fawned on her as if she had been gone for years.

'All right, all right,' Beth soothed as she picked up the little minx and cuddled the soft black fur against her cheek. 'All right—Pansy.'

Her dog replied by licking her nose. He didn't seem the least bit concerned by the name-change. 'So let's go home, Pansy,' Beth announced. Reinforcement, that's what one calls such things in school-teaching parlance. Reinforcement. Keep repeating the thing over and over again. Maybe *somebody* will believe it! *Pansy*?

So that was the way of it as Beth Hendley drove carefully down Palestine Road and over to West Canal, where

Henry Crosby, the loan officer at the First National Bank—no, not a member of *the* Crosby family—was sympathetic, but not too helpful. 'We hardly ever make loans to pay prospective court fines,' he finally offered, 'but your house is free and clear, Beth. We *could* make you a loan based on a mortgage of the premises. On the other hand, your sister——'

'No, I couldn't expect her to pay,' Beth said, sighing. One of the difficulties about living in a small town was that everyone knew your business. Every little detail. Like, for instance, that your stepsister had inherited all the money. 'I'll try to think of something else,' she told the banker. 'And if I can't, perhaps I'll be back about the mortgage.'

Outside in the car she sat rigidly behind the wheel, fighting her demons. Miss Beth Hendley, the iron hand in the velvet glove at school, but sitting here outside the red brick bank building, a lost, lonely soul with only her Fang—Pansy—to love her. And that's what I need, she told herself. Somebody to love me. Some *man* to love me. Who? The trouble with her job was that all the good men working at the school were happily married. And Picayune itself was not exactly overrun with eligible bachelors. She had accumulated a few male friends in the church organisations, dated a few boys in her student days, but nothing since graduating from university. Have I left it too long? That thought frightened her. She fumbled with the ignition key, and headed for home.

The front porch was shadowed as she drove up and parked in front of the garage. 'Now watch yourself, Pansy,' she instructed as she shifted to get out of the car. Naturally, with her arms full of dog, her skirt hiked up to further than that, and there was Frank Wylie, sitting up on her porch-swing, getting a good view. It was hard to tell whether she blushed or raged. The result was the same. Her cheeks turned red as she gritted her teeth and struggled up the stairs.

'You again,' she muttered. Her dog struggled to get down, but Beth held on. There was no way she could survive another biting. 'You don't have a home of your own?'

'Friendly,' he drawled. 'That's what I like about neighbours. Friendly. And here I went to the trouble of coming over here to apologise.'

Beth's foot stopped in mid-air. 'Apologise?'

'Yes.' He came up off the swing in a graceful arc and moved towards her. She could feel the pressure as he invaded her personal space. Hesitantly, facing him, with her dog in between, she felt with one heel for the doorstep behind her. 'You don't know the word?'

'I know the word,' she said, giving each word a distinct pronunciation. 'But I don't know the deed.' He moved an inch or two closer. 'Don't do that,' she protested. 'Fang—I mean, Pansy might—he might!'

'Pansy? Lo, how the mighty are fallen. I'll take that chance.'

'Don't be sarcastic. The—er—police department suggested I change his name. Which deed did you want to apologise for?'

'Which deed? You keep a long list of my transgressions, do you?'

'To tell the honest truth,' she exploded, 'yes. I'm listening.'

'Lucky me. Look, I apologise for picking on your dog. He had an interest, I suppose, that made him dig. I've taken care of that. I would appreciate, however, if you would keep—Pansy——' he was unable to mask the laughter '—if you would keep the animal out of my yard.'

'Thank you,' she muttered as she tried to butt open the door with her fundament. His hand streaked by her and turned the knob. She squeaked in surprise, and had to swallow hard to regain control. 'I would think you'd apologise for kissing me,' she challenged him.

'Not a chance. Apologies are for things I regret. I don't regret that, not the slightest bit. In fact, I'm thinking of doing it again!'

'Don't you ever-loving double-dare to.' Beth stepped up, going backwards, missed the threshold with one heel, teetered back and forward for a second, and fell into his arms. Fang growled. Before the dog could bite—if he intended to—Beth dropped him on to the veranda floor. But there was no escape for her. Frank Wylie's arms locked around her. 'Don't you dare,' she said, lifting her face up towards him.

Two strikes and you're out, she thought desperately. There seemed to be nothing else worth doing but to hang there like a great big rag doll and see what would come next. So she did.

There was a little more substance to *this* kiss. Helpless, she clung and let it happen. It was impossible to make a dispassionate study; her nerves all jangled at her, setting up a road-block in her brain. Mindless, she did her best to hang on until it was over.

'Well,' he said, and gently lowered her until her feet touched the floor. The dog whined, and jumped up on him, trying to lick his hand. He cleared his throat. 'Very well indeed,' he added. 'Did they have this on the curriculum at the University of Mississippi?'

Too many questions. How did *he* know I graduated from Ole Miss? Where did he learn to kiss like that? Am I going to spend the rest of my life being turned on by a man I can't stand? There were no sensible answers, but at least her pulse-rate was dropping. She took it out on her dog.

'Traitor,' she muttered.

Fang moved away a couple of steps, and then, with his tail between his legs, rushed into the house.

'Don't blame the dog,' he said quietly. 'It's all my fault.'

'You're darn well right it is,' she told him as she struggled to hold her back stiff, her face inscrutable. That's what I need, she thought. Some inscrutability. All those old black and white Charlie Chan moves. I need to pay more attention when I watch them. Inscrutable Beth Hendley. She shrugged her shoulders and glared at him.

'Don't let me keep you from anything,' she said. 'I'm sure you have a million things you'd rather be doing. You have apologised for *one* of your transgressions, so there's no reason for you to hang around. Goodbye, Mr Wylie.'

'Like to have me leave, would you?' That laughter was in his voice, overflowing.

'Yes, I would. Intensely. I intend to pray for you on Wednesday night at prayer meeting. Goodbye.'

He shook his head dolefully. 'I could probably use the prayers, Beth, but you've struck out completely tonight. Your sister invited me to supper again.'

Her mind was still not razor-sharp. What to say? Nothing came to mind. Nothing suitable, that is. She turned on her heel, offering a disgusted 'Inconceivable' over her shoulder, and let the screen door slam behind her as she went into the house.

Sue-Ann was waiting for her in the kitchen, her fingers nervously tapping on the solid square table in the middle of the room. 'Did you—rescue the dog?' Sue-Ann looked uncertainly at Beth, almost as if she expected an explosion. And she's going to get it, Beth told herself grimly. Her childhood is over. At twenty, Sue-Ann Foster has reached the end of the line.

'Yes, I rescued my dog.' Beth walked over in front of her taller sister and stood there, feet slightly apart, hands on hips. 'And let me tell you something, *sister*. Sit down.'

Sue-Ann collapsed into one of the kitchen chairs, folding her hands on top of the table. 'What?' she asked hesitantly.

'The party's over,' Beth snapped. 'I officially declare you grown-up and mature. Sukey, if you ever unchain my dog, or do anything else stupid like that again, I'm going to break your head. You understand me?'

'You shouldn't have kissed my man,' Sue-Ann said stubbornly.

'I told you once, and I'll tell you again,' Beth growled. 'I didn't kiss him. He kissed me. If you want to know why, go ask him. But whether or not, don't you forget. You do anything to cause my dog trouble from now on, and I'm going to break your head. And after that I might just let my fingernails grow and disarrange that beautiful face of yours. Got it?'

The two of them were almost nose-to-nose, with Beth leaning over, and Sue-Ann doing her ineffective best to back away. The montage held for a moment, and then the younger girl surrendered. 'Yes, I've got it. But you'll be sorry, Beth Hendley. Some day you'll be sorry.'

'Grow up,' Beth ordered as she stood up. 'That "you'll be sorry" bit was great when you were fifteen, but that's all behind you now.' With that, Beth whistled up her dog and took him out into the back yard, along with his food dish.

Night was beginning to close in. The bluebirds and English sparrows were stilled. In the distance she could hear the sound of a diesel engine over on the Southern Railroad tracks paralleling Main Street, splitting the little town in half. A breath of air curled around the maple trees that shaded the back yard, and filtered the odours of a country autumn into her nostrils. The outdoor world soothed her. Fang—Pansy—was busy at his dish, just as if he were the most law-abiding animal in all of Pearl River County.

Beth stretched, and then ran her fingers through her soft, thick hair, lifting it up off her neck so the breeze could properly do its job. Then, relaxed, she walked quietly back into the kitchen. Sue-Ann was still at the table, looking as if total disaster had struck. Beth was unable to stifle the pang in her heart as she looked at her helpless sister. Her anger had passed. Sukey had more troubles than the average bear, and deserved to be supported. 'What is it?'

'There's nothing in the refrigerator,' Sukey half whispered. 'I invited him to supper and there's nothing in the fridge. Look, Beth, you've got to run over to the market and get me some steak. Or chicken, maybe.'

'Not a chance, love. We shot the rest of the month's food budget on your beef Wellington the other day. I barely have enough for bread and milk to the end of the month. How about if you use some of *your* money and *you* dash over to the market? I'll keep your boyfriend in hand until you come back.'

Sue-Ann struggled to her feet. 'I—can't do that. I've already spent all my income for the month. Every cent.'

'As I remember, once again you didn't offer me anything for food or household expenses,' Beth commented mildly. 'How could you possibly spend it all?'

'I—ordered a new car.'

'Well! So there you go.' Beth dropped into the nearest chair and sighed.

'What do I do?' Sue-Ann tried her most appealing look, but this one day had torn some of the veils from

Beth's eyes, and she recognised what she saw. Her step-sister was an egocentric, spoiled woman, trying to make her way in the world on charm and good looks. Well, not with me, Beth told herself. Not any more. But she knew it wasn't true.

'I suppose you could always tell your hero that he'll have to go home and eat out of his own larder?'

'No! I couldn't do that!'

'In that case you'll have to make do with what we have.' Beth got up and went over to the refrigerator. 'There's plenty of cheese. Plenty of milk, too, for that matter. An egg or two. And tuna fish up on the shelf. Three or four cans of it. Bread—we've a loaf of bread left. Surely you could make something for him?'

'I—Beth?' Those big blue eyes glistened hypnotically. Try as she might, Beth was unable to throw off the appeal.

'All right,' she muttered. 'Go entertain the man. I'll whip up a Welsh rarebit. Beggars can't be choosers.'

'It—doesn't sound very attractive,' Sue-Ann muttered. 'But——' A smile flashed across the distressed face. She's thought of something, Beth told herself. And whatever it is, I'll bet I won't like it! 'OK,' Sue-Ann announced. 'I'll go tell him.' And with that she flounced out of the room, skipping.

'If I live to be a hundred,' Beth muttered, 'I'll never understand women. Especially me. Or men either, for that matter.' But there was a simple goal ahead, one that required only a *little* thought. She took a minute to let the dog back in. Fang settled in a corner of the kitchen, his eyes following her as she moved around the kitchen.

Welsh rarebit was perhaps not the hardest meal to prepare. It really was an elaborate presentation of cheese on toast. Beth whipped out her greaseless frying-pan, let the spoonful of butter melt, then broke pieces of cheese up into tiny balls and added them to the butter. Being a true Cajun cook, she added cayenne pepper and a few other spicy condiments which were readily at hand, and then, as the whole mess melted, she dropped bread into the toaster, beat the egg and milk together in a separate bowl, and added it to the pan. One minute was enough. She set out plates, and stepped to the door to call Sue-Ann.

There was no need for calling. Her sister came in, dragging Frank Wylie by the hand. 'Oh, did you go to all that trouble?' Sue-Ann asked innocently. 'Frank and I have decided to go out to supper. He feels like eating seafood, and——'

'Now, I didn't mean to cause you all that trouble,' Frank said as he came over to the stove and sniffed. 'Smells nice.'

'Oh, it's no trouble,' Beth said flatly. 'No trouble at all. Just a little cheese thing I whipped up.' Which has used up all the cheese on hand for the week, and pay-day eleven days away, she thought grimly. I'd like very much to let it cool for a minute and dump it all over his head!

'Of course it's no trouble,' Sue-Ann warbled. 'Come on, Frank. I know the nicest place for seafood. We'll drive down to Slidell, and...' The rest of the words faded as the pair of them left the kitchen.

Beth carefully turned off the gas, gently poured the rarebit over the toast on the plates, looked all around the room to be sure everything was safe and secure, and then, with a yell that could be heard—well, at least in the empty house next door, she shook the pan by its handle and then set it firmly back on the gas burner. She shuddered, struggling to control herself. The frying-pan, if she had thrown it where she'd intended, would have struck something of value—the glass-covered sampler that hung on the wall, made by her mother all those years ago.

'A woman's good conscience is a continual feast,' it quoted, 'and a quiet mind cureth all!'

'I'll kill them. Both of them,' she muttered as she pushed the dishes aimlessly around the table. 'Well, at least him! Fang!'

She snapped her fingers and pointed. The young dog, who admired table-scraps more than anything else in the world, jumped up on to a chair and put his forepaws on the table. 'Another no-no,' Beth groaned. 'I'm falling apart! I used to be a nice person to know! Now look at me!'

Her dog did just that, adding a little bark to the conversation. Beth shook her head at her own terrible manners and pushed one of the plates over in front of the dog, and sat down by the other. The dog struggled to find a place to begin. Beth did the same. Fang whined in frustration.

The cheese dish had cooled. Still in the daze that followed her rage, she picked up knife and fork and cut the dog's portion into little bites. Fang fell to with vigour. Beth tucked her chin down on to her palms, with her elbows on the table, and watched. Fang. Pansy. Frank Wylie. Life was too confusing. The only truth was that the sun would come up tomorrow morning, students would flock into the school, lesson plans would be followed, and nobody except herself would give one little toot about a teacher who was walking in a dream.

'Damn that man,' she muttered as she picked up her utensils and hacked at her rarebit. You don't have to talk the way Wylie does, her conscience dictated. Swearing is not ladylike!

'Neither am I,' she muttered as she struggled with her cold dinner.

CHAPTER THREE

THERE was this to be said about school teaching. Every day had a placid sameness about it, but there were tiny differences. One day brought a smile of understanding from some student who had been up the educational creek without a paddle for a week, the next found a sparkling sentence or two in an essay that hinted at depths unplumbed, on another one received a comforting word from some towering young man-child who seemed to recognise that teachers became tired, hurt, crotchety beyond their means. All these followed after each other in the pursuit of days, and suddenly it was Friday again.

'TGIF,' Margaret Lewis, the principal, told Beth as they passed in the hall just before the last period. 'Thank God it's Friday. Working your magic again, Beth?'

Because they were in the hall, and passing students were all ears, Beth clung to some formality. 'Magic, Ms Margaret?'

'Larry Lee. I understand he's passing all his subjects this quarter. Coach says he's a fine athlete, and the boy attributes it all to your tutoring. Guilty?'

Beth grinned. 'Guilty as charged, ma'am.'

'This isn't *High Noon*,' the principal chided. 'Don't be late for class.'

'I wouldn't dare,' Beth said.

'And Beth,' the principal added, 'Dr Wylie is working up a full head of steam, and needs some assistance. I wish that you help him out whenever you can.'

'*Dr* Wylie?' She had asked the more innocuous question. What she would have preferred to say was 'Me?

50

With that man?' But principals were in charge of things, even in the most informal of schools, and diplomacy triumphed.

'You didn't know? Of course. He was awarded his Ph.D. from Tulane last spring. Fine man, that. You'll certainly enjoy working with him. Better move along, dear. I can feel the bell's about to ring. Don't forget Dr Wylie.'

'Yes,' Beth said glumly. 'I mean, no, I won't forget.' Ms Margaret smiled at her again and bustled down the hall. 'Yeah,' Beth muttered. 'I'm sure I'll enjoy it. Like a case of typhoid fever I'll enjoy it!'

'Hurry up,' one of her students said as he whisked by her into the classroom. 'You wouldn't want to be the only one late for class!'

Blushing, Beth escaped from the hall. Her advance class was already seated. There was a muted buzz running around the room. Beth took one quick check at her lesson plan and her attendance chart. '1492,' she announced.

Immediately the refrain came back. 'Columbus sailed the ocean blue.'

'Nonsense,' Beth said, chuckling. 'Lots of people sailed the ocean blue. Why is it that from the relatively unimportant voyage of Columbus came the colonisation of America? Columbus was only a catalyst. What *really* was the major occurrence of 1492?'

A class-wide groan. 'And we're supposed to find out?' Mary Thigpen asked.

'And you're supposed to find out. Here's a list of material reserved for you in the library.' And from then on the class ran on its own momentum until the last bell rang. Beth answered the final question or two, dealt with the problems of a couple of eager students crowding her desk, and suddenly it was quiet. She sat back in her chair and sighed. She was tired, and there was still the regular

Friday night football game to attend. And the papers of
two classes had to be graded. And mark-books had to
be brought up to date. And new lesson plans had to be
laid out for the following two-week unit. 'And *Dr* Wylie
needs help—hah! I need to wash my hair,' she muttered.

So when Frank Wylie came into the room with what
passed for a smile on his face, Beth swallowed a couple
of times and searched her conscience. 'Larry Lee,' he
announced without preamble. 'They're going to have him
start the football game tonight. We're going to *whelm*
the opposition with our passing game!'

'Whelm?'

'Well, I don't expect we'll *overwhelm* them, so I
thought that just *whelm* would be a suitable substitute.
Ms Margaret tells me that you are solely responsible for
his being able to play.'

'Me?' Beth gasped. His big face looked as if something pained him. Probably because he has to speak
nicely to me, she told herself.

'You,' he admitted not too enthusiastically. 'He can't
play if he's not passing his academics. And I am told
it's been your tutoring that brought him up to a seventy-
five per cent average.'

'More likely you should congratulate him,' she said
softly. 'He did all the work.'

He cleared his throat and recovered his aplomb. 'Too
bad we can't say the same for Billy Joe. A good running
game to back up a good passing game. That's the ticket
for a winning football season.' It was a chilling statement
that drained the pleasure out of the day. He looked down
at her, as she still sat at her desk, nodded his head a
time or two, and walked out of the room.

I'm not going to let him get to me, Beth told herself.
Not today. I'm just not going to allow that! But allow
it or not, he had got to her. So much so that the point

of her pencil snapped from the pressure she was applying. 'He seems to think that I'm personally responsible for Billy Joe's running a low average,' she told herself. And then, because she was innately honest, 'And there are a few other things.'

'Talking to yourself, Beth?' Ms Margaret, the school principal, had stuck her head through the open door. 'Don't let things get you down.'

'No, lord, no,' Beth blurted. 'But Billy Joe Mowbray——'

'Ah. The one lost sheep?'

Beth, who had been raised on bible study, smiled. 'I suppose I should be pursuing the ninety and nine,' she said, 'but—the boy thinks all he has to do is step out on to the football field to become an instant hero. I can't seem to make him believe that he has to conform to the system!'

'You just have to keep his nose to the grindstone,' Ms Margaret offered.

'I don't even know where the grindstone is,' Beth mused.

'For Billy Joe?'

'No, for...' Embarrassed as she realised where her tongue had led her, Beth stammered to a stop. And then her temper took over. 'Lordy, he doesn't even *come* to the games. The faculty supports everything that goes on in the school, and he doesn't even *come* to the games!'

'Frank Wylie?' the principal chuckled.

'Frank Wylie!'

A moment of silence separated them, and Ms Margaret grinned again. 'Says he's an incessant busybody. Says if he comes he won't be able to keep his finger out of the pie. The coaches pray that he *would* come. They claim they could use a dozen fingers like his!'

'What are you talking about? Finger in the pie? Him? He's probably about as useful around a football field as a 1928 Ford.'

'Bite your tongue,' Ms Margaret said, laughing. 'You're talking about a man who was a star in the National Football League for nine years. Frank Wylie knows more about football than practically anybody in the state!'

Beth kicked her chair back and stood up, her face as rosy a red as the Sherwin-Williams paint company ever produced. 'You're teasing me, ma'am?' There was a begging behind her words. Tell me it's not true. Tell me he's never stepped on to a football field. Tell me what a dud he is!

'All true,' the principal told her. 'He'll be in the Football Hall of Fame just any one of these days. Something wrong? You're not looking well suddenly, Beth.'

She was an old friend, the principal, who had coached Beth during her student-teaching days, and could understand frank speech. 'I think I'm coming down with a terminal case of foot in the mouth,' Beth announced glumly, and began stuffing papers and pens indiscriminately into her briefcase. Her head was spinning. She could hardly acknowledge Ms Margaret's departure. A professional football player? What in the world was he doing as assistant principal in the Picayune Memorial High School? The question bothered her all the way home, so much so that she almost fell over Mr Scruggs's Persian cat, who was sunning himself in the middle of the narrow pavement on Juniper Street.

'Get out of the way, you miserable monster,' she muttered, and despite her Baptist upbringing her foot itched. The big cat opened its green slit-eyes wide and stopped licking its paw.

'Ah, Miss Hendley.' Alvin Scruggs came down to the pavement in his slippers. 'I wanted to talk to you.'

Beth took a deep breath, almost swallowed her chewing-gum and managed a smile. 'Do you really, Mr Scruggs? I was just telling myself what a magnificent cat your Persian is.'

'Indeed he is.' Alvin Scruggs was all business in the office, but outside those walls he was a cat-lover, of that breed willing to believe anything good said about his cat. 'Pedigreed, you know. Blue-blooded, so to speak.'

'It must be nice,' Beth said, sighing. 'Mongrels have such poor manners, don't you think?'

'Indeed I do.'

'But lovable, of course. I love my little dog.'

'Why—er—yes, of course.' He cleared his throat. 'Not everybody is as lucky as I am.'

'No, of course not. But then, you're such a kindly man. I've heard people at the school speaking of you in that vein.'

'Ha-humph,' he ha-humphed, acting as if he couldn't see how heavily she was spreading the butter.

'But you wanted to speak to me, Mr Scruggs.'

'Ah—er—it was nothing important, Miss Hendley. You're late coming home.'

'Yes, papers, and counselling, and all. It eats up the time.'

'Then you go along, m'dear. I did want to make mention of your dog, but it's not important. Go along, now. Your cheerleaders performing tonight?'

'As always. Lovely cat. Goodnight, Mr Scruggs.' She scuttled down the street with both sets of fingers crossed, hoping that the school committee member wouldn't be having second thoughts—about dogs or schools or anything, for that matter. Just to prove she could do it, she jogged the last block and a half, and came up the driveway panting, her heavy briefcase bouncing uncomfortably off her side. Fang set up an uproar from the back yard.

'Hey there, mutt,' she challenged him as she came around the side of the garage. The dog was up on his hind legs, held back by the long chain, his body wriggling as if it were boneless. 'C'mon, Pansy, settle down.' Fang had already forgotten his renaming. Beth finally smothered him against her, unfastened the chain, and carried the animal under one arm as she went into the kitchen. Immediately his claws hit the floor the dog made a mad dash for the water dish.

'What's the matter?' Beth followed along behind. The dog had an outdoor water dish which she had filled in the morning; now he acted as if he hadn't had a drink all day. 'What's the matter?' The dog continued to slurp up water.

Suspicious, Beth dropped her briefcase on the table and went back outside. The dog's outside dish was dry as a bone. 'And I'm sure I filled it,' she muttered as she went back into the house. 'I'm positive I filled it!' She was shaking her head when her sister popped in.

'Beth! What are we having for supper?'

'I don't know, love. There isn't much to choose from. Tuna fish salad, I suppose. I don't have a lot of time. We're playing at Long Beach tonight.'

'That's all you think of,' her sister said querulously. 'That school! You might as well be married to it!'

'You're probably right,' Beth admitted. 'It would be mighty uncomfortable in bed, though, with all that brickwork!'

'Beth!'

'Only joking. Only joking.' Beth clamped down on her runaway mouth. Sukey never did understand jokes, or jokers. 'Did you have a good day?'

'Not really. I went to a meeting of the library committee.'

'A worthwhile enterprise,' Beth commented as she went over to the shelf and began sorting through the available food selection.

'Don't poke fun at me,' her sister said in a strained voice.

Beth wheeled around. Sukey, who could cry on request, was trying to work up a storm. 'I wasn't poking fun,' she said. 'That's important work, sitting on the library committee. Time-consuming, too.'

'Well, *he* doesn't think so!' There was no need to discuss which *he* it was. Mr Boy Next Door, the estimable Frank Wylie. And when her sister needed defending, Beth was the type of woman to jump in with both feet.

'What has he said, Sue-Ann?'

'He said that everyone ought to have some meaningful work in life, and not just be a social parasite!'

Beth could have written the book about parasites, and her sister in particular, but to have that insufferable *man* make a statement like that was absolutely beyond the pale! 'Why, that—rotten man! He said that! Did you slap his face?'

'Oh, no, I wouldn't do anything like that.' Sue-Ann had got the tears flowing. A major flood was forecast. Beth hurried around the table and put her arms around her bigger sibling.

'Well, you should have,' she murmured. But I wouldn't. I wouldn't dare. He'd probably slug me back, that rotten—man! 'You need to ignore that sort of thing, Sukey. What does *he* know?'

'Well, I'm going to, Beth. I'm going to.'

'Going to what?'

'Going to go to work.'

'You?'

'You don't have to sound so—doubtful. I've been offered a job out at the Space Center.'

Oh, lord, Beth thought. As if the Space Agency doesn't have enough trouble, they're going to employ Sue-Ann at the Stennis Space Center? The world should tremble! 'What—what sort of job?'

'With Pan Am,' her sister said, turning off the flood. 'I'm going to be a tour guide and wear that lovely blue uniform, as if I were a stewardess or something, except I won't have to fly—you know that aeroplanes scare me!' Her voice ran down the scale as she ran out of breath.

'I know, love. That sounds like a *wonderful* job.' And how much damage could a tour guide do to the national space programme? 'When do you start?'

'Monday morning. I start the training programme on Monday. I'll show him—won't I, Beth?'

'You certainly will, love.' All the habits of her surrogate motherhood came back as Beth soothed the younger girl with practised skill, manoeuvred her to a chair at the kitchen table, and went about throwing a light but attractive meal together out of left-overs.

Later, as she watched her stepsister, her blonde head bent over her plate, Beth shook her head. It had been a long time since her mother had left a thirteen-year-old in her care. Seven long years. A frightened thirteen-year-old child. And sometimes, even now, the world seemed to be too much for Sue-Ann. Beth was still day-dreaming as she cleared the table, fed the dog, and took—Pansy— out for his compulsory walk.

All of which brought her to six o'clock, and a need to hurry. She restored Pansy to his chain, double-checked his water bowl, and headed for the garage with her wool sweater over her arm. It could get a little chilly in Dobie Holden Stadium on a late September night.

Her Escort had been a second-hand purchase. The milometer read thirty thousand miles, but left the distinct impression that this was its second time around. So Beth was startled to find that it started up at the first ignition impulse. 'Well,' she congratulated herself as she gently caressed the steering-wheel. 'Good girl!' The car burped a time or two, and settled down to a busy hum. Smiling broadly, Beth shifted into reverse and coaxed the tiny vehicle out of the garage and down the driveway.

There was little traffic on Third Avenue, but she paused, her rear wheels in the gutter, just in case. Just in case some idiot came roaring down the avenue as if it were a race course. Living near a school left that sort of precaution in an adult mind. And suddenly that marvellous engine stopped running. Stopped cold! Came to a complete stop, and ignored all the impatient jabs she gave it with the ignition key. Stopped cold, and obviously had no intention at all of carrying her a foot further!

'Darn!' she exploded, pounding on the wheel. 'Double-dyed darn, dipped in sheep-do!'

'Having a little trouble, are we?' If she had been set adrift, all alone, in a leaky boat, Beth told herself, this would be the last rescuer she would ever want to meet. But on the other hand, he might well be the *only* rescuer to come down the pike.

'Yes.' She managed to sweeten the word. 'My car— it doesn't seem to want to run. I don't suppose...?'

'No, I don't,' he answered cheerfully. 'I don't know a thing about automobiles. Too bad.'

'Yes, isn't it?' she muttered, doing her best to suppress the sarcasm. What use was a man who couldn't fix your car once and again? Instantly her over-feverish imagination began to provide her with a list of just such men, none of whom were as young or looked as nice as Frank Wylie. She blushed and ducked her head.

'Going some place important?'

'Poplarville.'

'Not too far. Why not borrow your sister's car?'

'You need to have your head examined if you think my sister would loan me her car,' she grumbled as she tried the ignition key one more time. 'Sukey wouldn't loan her car to the president of the United States if he asked.'

'You won't have a battery if you keep doing that.'

'Thanks a lot. For a man who knows nothing about cars you're pretty free with your advice.'

'Yes.' A big grin creased his face. 'I'm only trying to help, you know. What's going on at Poplarville?'

'A football game.' She struggled out of the car and slammed the door behind her. 'The Picayune Maroon Tide is playing the Hornets.'

'Ah. And you have a friend involved with the football programme, huh?' There was a little more sympathy in the words. Don't give up yet, she told herself as she reached back in the car for her sweater. Maybe he can be wheedled.

'Yes, you could say that.'

'I suppose I could drive you up there. Just you and I, riding through the moonlight?'

'I doubt if the moon would be up until after nine o'clock,' she murmured, all practicality. 'But it would be wonderful if you could see your way clear to——'

Watch it, her conscience dictated. Too much syrup and he'll get suspicious about the whole affair. She looked up at him. Something was tugging at the corner of his mouth. 'Of course,' he agreed. 'But your car is sticking out into the traffic lane. Suppose I steer while you push it up the incline a few feet.'

'You'll steer? I'll push?'

'Dammit, did I get that backwards?' One of his big hands ushered her back into the driving seat, and shut the door behind her.

As he strolled around to the rear of her car she could hardly help muttering, 'And you needn't curse!'

She could feel the car jerk and then fall back into its original position. Two more tries, and no advance had been made at all. She shivered as she slumped down in the seat and watched in her outside mirror. He straightened up and came stalking back up beside her. Both his hands appeared on the door, and his head came about as close as she could stand.

'Do you suppose,' he asked softly, 'that you could release the hand brake?'

'I—er——' Her hands fumbled. The release handle seemed to have a mind of its own, but finally it slid forward and disengaged. 'I——'

'I understand,' he said gently. But as he walked away she thought she heard him mutter derisively, 'History teachers!' Then he called, 'Ready?'

'All ready!' Beth yelled. How could I not be ready? He must think he's dealing with Mississippi's prize dolt. She checked the gear shift to be sure it was in neutral, and this time the car moved back up the drive as if another motor had been attached.

'The brake!' he yelled.

'Brake. Yes,' she muttered. 'Damn the man. Oh, I shouldn't have said that! Or maybe I should have. He's enough to tempt a saint from his prayers!'

'You could get out now,' he suggested. 'Unless you've given up the idea?'

'No—no,' she mumbled as she swung out of the car. Her mind was working overtime. Here I am, one of the world's *practical* young women—well, scratch that *young* bit—and yet every time this man comes close to me I seem to come unglued! 'No, indeed, I *have* to go.'

'So come along.' He had one hand under her elbow, hustling her along as if she were a prisoner. The front door of the house behind her opened.

'Beth? What are you doing to Frank?'

'Me?' Beth protested. 'I'm not doing anything, Sue-Ann. Ask him!'

'I'm taking your sister for a little ride,' Frank Wylie called. 'Don't worry, I'll bring her safely back.'

'I—don't think that's what she wanted to hear,' Beth panted. They were already around the end of the hedge, and were struggling up his drive. That was, Beth was struggling. Frank was moving along with all the aplomb of a sternwheeler on the river. The Mississippi River, of course.

'We'll take my Mercedes,' he announced as he opened the front right-hand door and shoved her in.

'Yes,' she gasped. 'Of course, doesn't everyone?'

'What?' He had come around the front of the car. The vehicle seemed to tilt as he climbed in and sat down.

'Nothing,' she stammered. 'I'm sure we'll—I'll—enjoy it. I've never ridden in a Mercedes before.'

'And what's that about your sister?' The engine purred under his command as he competently guided the car out into the street.

Beth settled back against the soft leather, and managed to relax. 'About Sukey? What about her?'

'She seems to have a strange personality,' he offered as he guided his car up the boulevard and stopped at the school. 'Directions?'

'Just—follow those school buses,' Beth advised, and ducked back into the corner darkness to hide the expression on her face.

But he was persistent. When they reached the highway he prompted her again. 'Your sister?'

'I—I'm glad you spoke to her about working,' Beth said at high speed. 'She's going to work on Monday, and I'm sure it will be good for her. She doesn't need the money, of course, but——'

'She needs a little discipline,' he interjected as he pulled over to the kerb in front of the school. 'A lovely girl.' He turned to look in her direction. There was a satisfied look on his rugged face. 'I'm glad to have this opportunity to be alone with you. We have a number of things to talk about.'

'Yes, well...' she said, nervously licking her dry lips. 'I'm glad to see that you and Sukey are getting along so nicely, Mr Wylie. She needs——'

'Frank,' he interrupted. 'Call me Frank.'

'Er—yes. Frank.' It wasn't as hard to say as she had expected. But his big hand came over and patted her knee, and she jumped.

'She's a fragile creature,' he mused. 'Beth?'

'Well, she's had a life full of difficulties.' Beth was off on her favourite subject, her sister. 'She needs caring concern.'

'And what does Beth Hendley need?' he asked softly. His eyes were straight ahead on the road. Beth stared at his dark profile. What does Beth Hendley need?

'Nothing,' she finally answered. 'Beth Hendley is a tough cookie who can look out for herself. Sukey needs——'

'You'd do anything in the world for that woman, would you?'

'Of course. She's twenty years old, and she's been my sister for eighteen years. How could I not love her, help her? Some day she'll meet the right man, who will take her away, and after *that* I can worry about what Beth Hendley needs.'

He took his eyes off the road for a moment and stared at her. In the dull darkness Beth almost thought she could see a frown on his face, but the moon was not yet up, and the highway had few lights. Change the subject! she told herself fiercely. Now!

'Tell me about you,' she asked. He gave her another quizzical look, and a chuckle.

'Quick-change artist, huh?' There was a moment of silence as he mustered his thoughts. 'Actually there's not much to tell. My father was a coalminer in West Virginia. He died young. Black lung disease. My mother disappeared a couple of years later, and my Aunt Harriet raised me. You'll have to meet her some day. Now there's a *real* tough cookie. Is that the stadium up ahead there?'

It was cool in the stadium. As darkness fell the Mississippi heat escaped with a rush, driven by a northeast breeze. Frank Wylie helped her to a seat in the bleachers. 'Should have brought a blanket,' he called as he helped her up the cliffside of open benches.

'I—have to go down on the field for a minute,' she told him as she tried to tug her hand free. It was a difficult job. First, because he was a strong man, and second, because things felt altogether—agreeable.

'So you're the sponsor of the cheerleading squad?'

'Well, somebody has to,' she said. 'It's not all zis-boom-bah these days. There's a lot of gymnastic work involved, and a number of routines, and—and I won't get anything done if you don't turn me loose, Mr Wylie. That is, Frank. Please?'

'Now that I like,' he said, chuckling. 'OK, go do your bit. Want some popcorn?'

'Do I ever. My stomach feels as if it's been cut off from the mainstream of life for hours!'

Rhonda, the head cheerleader, had the squad gathered around her. The football team was using half the field for warm-ups, and the Picayune Marching Band was putting on an exhibition on the other half. The noise was halfway between storm and utter destruction.

'Got yourself a live one, Ms Beth,' Rhonda commented. 'And he's the assistant principal? Heavens to Betsy!'

'I haven't—*got him*,' Beth snapped. 'He's just—a man with a car when I needed a ride. Now, does everyone have the sequences?'

'I'd rather have *him*,' Rhonda insisted. 'I wonder if he'd wait a year or two? Being sixteen is one terrible drudge!'

'And so is being——' Beth, who hated to admit how old she was in public, almost bit her tongue.

All the girls stared at her. 'Being?' Marie prodded.

'Being out in the cold,' Beth finished. 'It might rain tonight. We can't afford another flu attack. I'll be waiting for you at the ticket booth when the game's over. *And nobody wanders away by themselves!* Got it?'

Eight faces nodded solemnly, and at least seven minds went to work on the problem: how to escape the chaperon on Friday night. It was a course pursued in every high school in the nation. 'All right, then,' Beth yelled. 'Go get 'em, girls!'

She was talking to herself as she fought her way back up into the stands. The crowd was increasing. Neither team was likely to set a record, district or state-wise. So both teams—and their supporters—would come out head-hunting. Frank Wylie was sitting in approximately the same place, and had accumulated two large boxes of popcorn, two steaming hot cups of coffee set in a plastic tray, and one blanket marked 'Property of Athletic Department'. Beth looked and said not a thing.

He made a space for her at his side, then folded the blanket over her knees. 'I could have got two,' he confessed ruefully, 'but I didn't have the nerve. That equipment manager is one fierce young man. You were talking to yourself as you came up. Trouble with the young ladies?'

'It's a big stadium, they're a long way from home, it's going to be a dark, dark night, and they are eight healthy young women, sixteen going on twenty-five. No, there's no trouble.'

'But?' he teased.

'I'm sure you know,' she returned. 'But *anything* can happen, so it probably will. I can't run as fast as they can, I can't shout loud enough to be heard over the crowd, there'll be a hundred boys clustering around by the end of the game. So I have to out-think them.'

'Put them on the honour system, I suppose?'

'Oh, yes. And carry a big stick. Here comes the team.'

The popcorn was hot, the coffee was acceptable, the game was a confusion of heroics and errors, and by the end of the first half Picayune was trailing, seventeen to seven. Beth, who understood the game only in generalities, was hoarse from cheering. 'Say,' she told him as the whistle ended the half, 'I'm sorry I banged on your arm like that. I tend to get excited.'

'I can see that,' he commented, rubbing his upper arm. 'It didn't hurt much. I'm sure the bleeding will stop by morning. You're a different person out here, Beth Hendley.'

'Different? How different?'

'Full of spirit.'

'Aren't you enjoying the game?'

'And that's where you've got me,' he murmured. 'I've got an itch and can't scratch it.'

'What is it?'

'We can't win this game if we can't run the ball on the ground. Every time that number twenty-seven starts——'

'That's Billy Joe,' she interrupted.

He gave her a quick look, and shook his head. 'Every time Billy Joe heads around the left end of the line he gets creamed. I think their team must outweigh ours by forty pounds per man.'

'Poor Billy Joe,' Beth sighed. 'That monster on the other team just stands there waiting to murder him. Isn't somebody supposed to do something about that?'

'Somebody is,' Frank growled. 'That little guy who runs in front of Billy Joe. That number forty-eight.'

'Then I suppose we don't have a chance,' Beth mourned.

'Nonsense,' the big man grunted. 'Football's a game of inches. I could——'

'Well, if you're all that smart, why don't you?'

'The coach would kill me.'

'Try him,' she said, teasing. 'He hasn't murdered me yet, and I make all kinds of suggestions.' She stopped for a second to search his face out. 'Of course, the coaches do laugh a lot.' In the glare of the floodlights he seemed made of armoured bronze. Whistles blew out on the field, signifying the end of the first half of the game. Teams and officials trotted off towards the dressing-rooms under the bleachers.

'Damned if I won't,' he muttered. 'Hold my popcorn.' And with that he went bounding down the steps, two at a time, just in time to catch one of the assistant coaches before he disappeared into the locker-room.

So how is it possible, Beth asked herself, that I feel
so all alone in the middle of a crowd? What was the
name of that boy who was my last football date? Six
years ago? Or maybe only five? Henry. Henry something or other. Married now, I suppose. I wish I knew
what I've been looking for all these years. Or whom?
Certainly not Frank Wylie. I can't stand the man, and
yet—well, maybe it was the blanket he—borrowed?
Something's been keeping me warm! He's just the sort
of man that Sukey needs. If only he didn't curse so much!

The drill squads and the two bands filled the half-time
break. Just as the teams came out on the field again
Frank Wylie was back. Beth sighed in relief. She had
not been at all sure he would return, and the thought
had bothered her. He sat down, his weight rattling the
bleacher seat as he did so. For a second he squirmed—
closer, her discerning mind told her. Isn't that nice? She
flashed him a smile and handed him his popcorn bag.
The two teams lined up, the whistle blew, the Hornets
kicked off to the Picayune team, and the second half of
the game was under way.

'Somebody,' he said directly into her ear, 'ate my
popcorn. I said hold it, not eat it!'

'You just can't trust anybody these days,' she retorted,
and after that things became a little confused. He was
either kissing or biting her ear. The blanket was pulled
up and over them. Somehow one of his hands went
around her waist, and paused for purchase just an inch
or two below her breast. 'I don't——' she stammered,
just as the crowd roared and drowned everything out.

Somebody had given Billy Joe the ball and he dashed
for the left end of the line. The giant on the other team
stood up and waited, both arms extended. Even with his
mask on, his smile could be seen. Like Gargantua, he
positioned himself right in the path of the running ball-

carrier. And then, almost like a miracle, a hurtling body smashed into the giant below the knees. The big man tottered, side-stepped, and fell over like a massive bowling-pin. Billy Joe went through the hole the giant's fall had created, and several seconds later crossed the goal line at the far end of the field.

'How about that?' Frank Wylie said in a very self-satisfied tone.

'Why, that's—what did you do?' she asked.

'Who, me? I was sitting up here in the bleachers, minding my own business,' he said innocently.

'No,' she insisted. 'What did you tell them?'

'Football is a game of inches,' he repeated solemnly. 'The boy doing the blocking was attacking too high, and from the wrong angle. I wish you hadn't eaten my popcorn.'

'Why, that's wonderful,' Beth commented.

'The popcorn? It wasn't that good, but I didn't get any supper.'

'What the devil are you doing at a place like Picayune?'

'Earning my daily bread?'

'I don't believe that. Somebody told me you played in the National Football League. You must have made gobs of money! What *are* you doing *here*?'

'You ask a great many questions,' he told her, grinning. 'I'm conducting a national survey on the way girls respond to kissing at football games.'

'You can't do that,' she exclaimed. 'There's Sukey to consider!'

'Who?' he asked, and then he proceeded to demonstrate his kissing survey. Picayune lost the game by two points, but Beth Hendley was too dazed to notice.

CHAPTER FOUR

IT WAS surprising how two grown women could live in the same house and manage to avoid each other for days on end. It was Wednesday evening. Beth had stopped off at Evelyn's Restaurant for a light dinner, and then went on to Paul's Pastries, where she picked up a huge Boston cream pie to serve as dessert. Every now and again, when her troubles seemed insurmountable, she forgot her calorie-count. She was pigging it out when Sue-Ann wandered in.

They made a strange contrast. Beth was dressed soberly in a dark green blazer and skirt to match. A kitchen towel served as a bib, protecting the ruffled lace of her white blouse. Sue-Ann, with her long blonde hair awry, wore one of her lawn cotton négligés over what appeared to be nothing at all.

'Have a good weekend?' The younger girl strolled over to the counter and poured herself a cup of coffee.

'Marvellous,' Beth responded gloomily. The hearing in Municipal Court had included a lengthy lecture about citizens' rights and a fine of fifty dollars and costs, and had ended with the Olympian summary, 'School-teachers are supposed to set an example for the community!' Guilty or not, Beth hated to be the subject of lectures. But she had managed to suppress her wild temper on just this one occasion, and had driven home, muttering to herself.

'Marvellous,' Beth repeated. 'And you?'

'I'm not sure,' Sue-Ann murmured. 'This work stuff— it's harder than I thought. Did you know they expect you to be at the tourist desk at eight o'clock every morning—exactly on time?'

'Do they really?' Beth offered, halfway between sympathy and sarcasm. 'Every morning?'

'Every morning.' Sue-Ann sighed. 'And only a half-hour for lunch. It's very tiresome.'

'I'll bet it is.' Habit had spilled all over caution, the way chocolate syrup smothered the scoop of ice-cream. Beth had for so long been Sue-Ann's surrogate mother that she was almost sorry for the child. After all, although *she* couldn't remember that far back, the first day of labour was the last day of childhood. 'But it will get easier as it goes on,' she said.

'No, it won't,' Sue-Ann returned. 'I was conducting a tour out by the engine-firing gantries, and a darn alligator wandered up and scared me half to death. I could hardly get back on the bus.' A brief pause to see what effect *alligators* had on her sister. None at all, to tell the truth. The monsters were a protected species, and occasionally they came wandering up from the swamps to look around. Seeing no result, Sukey continued. 'I think I've done enough to impress him, so I quit.'

'After three days?' Beth shook her head wearily. 'We're talking about Frank Wylie, aren't we?'

'Of course. He likes me because I'm beautiful. And it takes a long time every day to be beautiful. I've given this a lot of thought. I'm going to impress him with being a home-body. Don't you think——?'

'Yes, I'm sure that would impress him.' Beth hurried with her own coffee, and almost burned the tip of her tongue. Soap and water and a little lipstick were her beauty treatments. Oh, and twenty minutes every night brushing her hair. Could that be the reason she received only growls from Frank? 'Yes, I'm sure he'll notice.'

'I thought he would,' Sue-Ann continued, preening herself. 'Yes. I'll cook him some fine meals, and look domestic, and——'

'You bet.' Beth pushed away from the table. She had twenty minutes to get to prayer meeting, and had fallen from grace more than a time or two with her terrible temper lately, so the sarcasm escaped. 'Don't forget to vacuum under the beds, love.'

'*His* bed?'

'Why not?' Beth said as she walked out of the room. 'Whatever turns you on!'

'But I didn't plan to *do* anything,' Sue-Ann wailed. 'I just planned to *look* as if I was doing something.'

'There's always that,' Beth called, looking back over her shoulder. And as a result set foot on the veranda and bounced off a very large chest.

'You again?'

'Me again. Bad pennies, and all that.'

Beth decided to try the cautious approach. 'There's something wrong with your house? The roof leaks, or something?'

'Hard to tell,' he commented gravely. 'I haven't been home during a rainstorm yet. It would appear that you're going someplace?'

'How perspicacious of you,' Beth muttered. 'Sue-Ann is in the kitchen domesticating.'

He faked a shivery shrug. 'I don't intend to eat it. Why didn't you tell me that *you* cooked the beef Wellington the other night?'

'Look, I'm going to be late for church,' she protested, and managed to get to the foot of the stairs. Somehow or another she had managed to entangle her elbow with his hand, and it was stuck there despite her attempts to shake it off.

'So why didn't you tell me?' he persisted.

'Why should I tell you?' she huffed. 'Obviously someone else saved me the bother. Yes, I cooked your dinner, but you were lucky.'

'Lucky?'

'Lucky,' she stated very firmly. 'I really didn't know how rotten you were, and we were all out of garlic and hemlock juice at the time.'

'Hemlock juice? I can't believe that.'

'Believe it,' she muttered. 'Would you kindly turn me loose?'

'Don't believe I can,' he returned cheerfully. 'My hand seems to be stuck. And nobody told me. I finally figured it out for myself.'

'I'll bet you did. Some miracle occurred?'

'Don't be petty.' The rumble of his deep voice nudged at her nerves. If only he weren't such a large pain in the neck, he would be a wonderful fellow! she told herself. As in guy and girl, and walks in the moonlight, and—who knows?—maybe even love forever after?

But even as she thought she recognised the impossibility. Former football heroes chase after sophisticated blondes, or bubbly, healthy cheerleaders. They don't pal around with tired, elderly history teachers. So why is he haunting me?

'No, I finally figured it out for myself,' he repeated. 'The following day, when I tried to get all that flour off my coat. And then I remembered that *you* were the only one I had hugged that night.'

'And if I believed that you'd be willing to sell me a bridge,' she commented cynically. 'Unfortunately I've got to be gone. I've only ten minutes, and I have to walk. My car is up at Cowboy's garage. I think it's suffering from a terminal case of old age.'

'Walk? You can't walk across the boulevard. You know darn well that the place is overset with kid gangs.'

'They have to go somewhere,' she told him. 'Not that
I condone some of the things they do—and the curfew
has cut down some of the trouble—and now what are
you doing?'

'I'm walking you over,' he announced.

'Oh, how lovely,' she snapped. 'I don't need to be
walked over. It's still daylight. If anything, I'd be more
fearful of you than the gangs!'

'You didn't talk like this at the football game.'

'Yes, well, I had all those cheerleaders on my side.'
He winced, as if she had punctured both his hard head
and his ego, all at one blow. And all the while he was
propelling her down Glenwood Street. 'Nothing to say?'
she coaxed. 'I hope the roof of the church doesn't
collapse. You *are* coming in with me?'

'Oh, shh...sugar!' he roared. 'No, I'm not coming
in with you. The roof *would* fall down.' He grabbed at
her arm again, and hustled her along. It hurt, but she
refused to let him know. He would probably take it for
another sign of weakness!

She came out of church refreshed. Prayer and medi-
tation did that for her more often than not. The congregation gathered on the steps for a moment of gossip,
and then dispersed. Twilight had fallen, and under the
canopy of trees that lined Goodyear Boulevard she could
hear the sigh of the breeze, the song of the night birds,
the smell of September, now shredded down to its last
day. The huge pillars that were the architectural mark
of the church made towering shadows. And a smaller
shadow detached itself from the larger ones around it.

'It's about time,' Frank Wylie said in a gentle,
conversational voice. She could barely see his welcome
face.

'I didn't think you'd wait.'

'But you're glad?'

She shivered from the emotion of it all, not from the cold. Truth-time. 'Yes, I'm glad.' Said softly, almost a whisper, hardly heard above the rustling of the trees. His big hand took her elbow, gently this time. Is there such a thing as elbow-fetish? she asked herself, trying to restrain the giggle.

'So am I.'

They walked together. His arm dropped her elbow and went around her waist, pulling her close enough to make them one entity. He led her up the boulevard, rather than across. She made a muted protest.

'We're taking a long cut,' he told her.

'If you mean short cut, you're going the wrong way.'

'I know what I'm doing,' he said huskily. She sighed and smiled up at him. Thank the lord he knows what *he's* doing, she told herself, because *I* surely don't! And I'm glad. She inclined her head an inch or two, resting it on his very capable shoulder. He smelled of maleness and aftershave, and it felt so good to be wanted. They walked slowly, as if there were all the time in the world. Almost up to the hospital they ran out of trees. Across the open area she could see the lights of the library, the outline of the junior high school, the high school.

Parked against the central reservation of the boulevard there were three small open trucks. Cajun Cadillacs, they were known as in this corner of the South. Quarter-tonners, with multiple headlights and searchlights, kept as immaculate as their young owners could keep them.

'Something bothering you?' He pulled her to a stop.

'Yes,' she murmured. 'That boy. I think I know him.'

'Where?'

'Right over there. Leaning on the fender of that red truck.'

'Lives in this neighbourhood, does he?'

'Lord, no. He lives up on Stemwood Drive, if that's the boy I think it is. I have to talk to him.'

'Don't be a fool, Beth. You don't believe that bunch is just standing there making conversation? There are just as many drug-pushers and trouble-makers in Picayune as there are in any town in America!'

'I *have* to talk to the boy.' By dint of much struggle she managed to break free of him and ran out into the boulevard. The young men saw her immediately, and quickly dived into the trucks. Engines roared. The red vehicle jumped the kerb of the road divider, bounced down on to the south lanes where Beth now stood, hesitantly, and came directly for her with all its many lights blazing. She could see the face of the driver—Billy Joe Mowbray, his face distorted in—fear?

Beth had absolutely no control over her muscles. Like a fawn blinded by an illegal hunter's lights, she froze in position as the truck bounced down on to the pavement. The tyres squealed, and still she could not move. Could not, that was, until Frank Wylie came running up behind her, cursing. He snatched her up without stopping, angled away from the truck, and, in a rolling dive, landed them both on the grass of the divider.

The truck squealed to a stop, reversed itself, and roared up the road towards Main Street. Beth huddled up in a ball within the circle of Frank's arms, shaking madly. 'There, now,' he murmured as he stroked the hair out of her eyes. 'It's all over, love. He's gone.'

Moments later, as the shivering stopped, Beth's mind seized not on the attempt to harm her, but upon his words. 'It's all over, love.' *Love*? Maybe it's just an expression, or something. Maybe he means it, she thought. Maybe you're a bigger fool than you thought, her conscience dictated. Why would a man like this one want *you*? Insecure, stuck-on-the-shelf Beth Hendley had to agree. She relaxed her mind, and the myriad aches and pains all over her body began to report in.

Her shivering stopped. She sniffed away a couple of tears. Frank Wylie was lying protectively on top of her. Now he shifted his weight, and she whimpered at the loss. 'It's all right, Beth. What hurts?'

'Everything.' She managed a feeble little grin. 'I think everything is attached, but—my ego has been dented seriously. Thank you, Francis.'

'Francis?' He scrambled to his feet, and extended both hands in her direction. She locked on to them and he gently pulled her to her feet.

'Francis,' she said solemnly. 'It's a nice name. A very nice name. I might even use it from time to time.'

'Well, I'll be damned!'

'Probably, if you keep swearing like that. My foot hurts.'

'Ah. Well, we're only half a block from the hospital. We might as well——'

'No. I'm not hurt *that* much,' she interrupted. 'Just aches and pains and bruises.'

'We're going to the hospital,' he said. Moses might have spoken in the same manner when he'd come down from the mountain.

'Yes,' she said, sighing. And then, just to emphasise the height of her submission, 'Yes, sir.' He swept her up in his arms as if she were a bale of feathers, and started off up the street.

'Now let me understand this,' Sergeant Matthews said patiently. He was sitting on one of the high stools in the emergency-room, trying to balance his notepad on his knee. 'This truck came over the central reservation of the road and headed directly for you?'

'I—guess so,' Beth responded.

'Don't keep moving your leg,' the doctor ordered as he dabbed anti-bacterial lotion on the worst of her scratches.

'You don't know?' the sergeant asked.

'Well, things got to be pretty—ouch, that stings— hectic, you know. I didn't respond very well.'

'For heaven's sake, leave her alone,' Frank Wylie said angrily. 'Can't you see she's in a state of shock? Ask her tomorrow—or the day after.'

'All right,' the police sergeant said. 'Tomorrow. But we don't need any vigilantes in this town.'

'I'll bet you don't,' Wylie snapped. 'Just leave me alone with my—fiancée!' The sergeant gave him a disgruntled look and moved out of the emergency alcove, still consulting his notebook.

'Fiancée?' Beth asked cautiously.

Frank kissed her gently on the forehead. 'Just a subterfuge,' he whispered. 'Otherwise I might get thrown out of here.'

'But—fiancée? He's one of the wardens of my church.'

'Don't worry. It'll all blow over.'

'Yeah, sure,' she sighed. 'A lot *you* know about small towns!'

Beth winced as the doctor strapped up her ankle. There was nothing of greater interest to her young life than Frank's answer, but he seemed unwilling to expand on it.

'That won't be too bad, Beth,' the doctor announced. 'Just a few bangs and bruises. You'd do well to keep off that ankle for a day or two. It's only a sprain, but——'

'I can't do that,' she wailed. 'I have three new units to start in classes tomorrow.'

'You *can* do that,' Wylie interjected. 'You *will* do that!'

'Dictator,' she muttered under her breath.

'I have super-hearing,' he murmured. 'See that you do what you're told. That's the assistant principal speaking to you, that is.'

'I don't have to pay attention to assistant principals when I'm off duty,' she whispered. Whispered, because although she was stretched out flat on the trolley, he was bending over so closely that his lips were at her ear.

'You'd better watch out,' he replied. 'I've been known to eat little girls like you with one bite.'

Beth struggled up on to her elbows. 'Don't do that,' the doctor complained. 'Why is it that schoolteachers are such terrible patients? Fiancée, eh?'

'You'd find me very indigestible.' Beth glared up at Frank, and then paused for thought. He called me 'love'. He saved me from a very nasty accident. He's a terrible man, but...?

'Day off tomorrow,' Frank Wylie told her gently. 'I'll take your classes myself.'

And in the face of so many dictators, Beth surrendered. Her eyes glistened but a smile played across her face. 'If you say so—Francis,' she replied.

'Now about this driver,' Frank said as the doctor walked away. 'You can't give me a description?'

'No—I'm afraid not,' Beth told him, lying hard enough to squander her soul. She knew exactly who the driver was, but had no wish to saddle the boy with a police record. Not, at least, until she had talked to him about the incident. 'No. The street lights and the headlights, and all—I'm afraid all I could see was a sort of shadow.'

'But he was tall?'

'Medium tall.'

'Very tall,' Frank said. 'Almost as tall as I am. And the truck was a red quarter-ton with an open back?'

'I don't remember,' Beth said.

'You don't recall? And the right front tyre had some splashes of white paint across the rim?'

'I don't know.'

'But you saw the licence plate?'

'No, I didn't.' But he was getting too close to the truth; Beth closed her eyes and feigned sleep.

'Can't you see that the girl is on the edge of a trauma? This hasn't been any pink tea.' The doctor brushed him aside. 'Now, I want Ms Beth to relax for a while, and I'm going to give her something to help to do that.'

'She can go home tonight?' Frank elbowed the doctor aside as soon as he had withdrawn the needle, and picked up Beth's hand.

'Yes, she can go home tonight. Probably in a couple of hours, if she has someone to haul her out of here. You can wait in the lobby,' Dr Tuttle said, looking pointedly at Wylie.

'Not on your life,' Frank retorted. He pulled a stool up close to the trolley and sat down, still holding Beth's hand.

'Hey, if you're not a relative you can't stay,' the doctor insisted.

'So all right, I'm a relative,' Frank growled. 'She's my fiancée.'

'She doesn't look as if she believes it. I think I'm going to have to throw you out.' Dr Tuttle, who stood a bent five feet ten and might have weighed one hundred and ten pounds soaking wet, squared himself away.

'Don't,' Frank Wylie said. 'Somebody might get hurt, and I'm afraid it might be me. Tell him, Beth.'

'I'm very sleepy,' she said, yawning.

Frank stood up, towering over the doctor. 'Tell him you love me, Beth. Otherwise he's going to beat up on me.'

'In that case,' the girl said sleepily as the sedative smashed into her and released her inhibitions, 'yes, I love him very much, Doctor. Please?'

'I've never seen such goings-on in all my life,' the nurse said. 'Doctor, you've got another patient in booth four. Leave these two to me.'

'Hold my hand, Francis,' Beth murmured drowsily. 'She's bigger than the doctor.'

It was midnight when Frank Wylie drove up into Beth's driveway. She was awake, but just barely, her mind filled with delightful dreams. He came around to the passenger side, swung the door open, and scooped her up. She made no protest. It was beginning to be fun, being hauled around like a wrapped Christmas package. Fang was sitting on the front porch, unchained, shivering with anticipation.

'The damn door's locked,' Frank reported.

'Well, put me down,' she drawled. 'Sue-Ann must have gone to bed.'

'Her car's not out front,' he observed.

'Well, put me down,' she repeated, 'and I'll unlock the damn—oops—the door.'

'Catching, isn't it?'

'Don't be a—pushy guy,' Beth managed. Her mind was thinking up hundreds of words, but her teeth seemed to be fixed in place and wouldn't let them jump out. 'It must be that shot he gave me. I can't seem to——'

'Lean against me,' he coaxed as he set her down on her own feet. 'Now, the key?'

'Always put the key in my pocket,' she murmured. 'Key in pocket. Francis Scott Key. In my pocket?'

'Oh, boy. Hold on, lady.' She leaned against him. His arms went around her, and began to pat certain protruding areas.

'No pockets in my skirt,' she muttered. The hands shifted, coming around to search in her blazer. Two pockets, no key.

'Inna blouse,' she managed. The hands moved again, peeling back the blazer, tugging at the single tiny pocket just over her breast. There was an inordinate amount of fumbling around, all in the wrong places. Or maybe in the right places, she thought. Well, anyway, in places to which she had never ever invited search routines. 'Can't finum?' she mumbled.

'What?'

'Keys? Can't finum?'

'Oh, keys. Yes, I found them. Lovely.'

'Lovely keys?'

'Damn. Hang on while I try the lock.'

'Mmmmm.'

She locked both her hands around his neck as he leaned forward. Her dog was jumping, trying to get high enough to lick her. 'C'mon, mutt,' he muttered, 'give me a break.' That arm went under her knees again, and she was airborne. He fumbled for another minute or two, and the overhead lights came on. 'Which room?'

'Down hall. End room. Too heavy?'

'You? Too heavy? Why, you hardly weigh enough to write home about.'

'But breathing hard!'

'My panting has nothing to do with your weight. Hush up, now. Talking uses a lot of necessary air.'

'Necessary air. Write home about?' Things seemed so funny that she started to giggle. The world was round and red and rosy. Flares of rainbows sprang up in her mind, and then faded away. The pain had gone, every bit of it. 'Bed,' she commanded.

'Right. Bed.' He lowered her gently to the surface of the bed, and his arms withdrew. She felt immediate regret. Warmth had disappeared along with the arms; warmth and good cheer and happiness. She whimpered, and he was back at her side again.

'Easy does it,' he said. 'Sue-Ann's not home, that's for sure.'

'I don't care,' she muttered. 'Big girl now.'

'You?'

'S-Sue-Ann. Silly name. Whatcha doin' now?'

'I'm going to put you to bed,' he announced. 'If your dog will let go of my shoe.'

'Fang! Sit!' she commanded. To everyone's surprise Fang moved out of the way and sat still. Her eyes closed. Frank was looking for the key again. His big fingers tugged at the tiny pearl buttons of her blouse, and suddenly it was gone. One hand slipped under her buttocks as he pulled the blanket down. Her slip seemed to be tangled with the gold locket around her neck, and then both of them were gone. And still he hadn't found the keys.

'Nothin' there,' she mumbled. He laughed.

'There's more there than any man might need, love.'

'Cold,' she sighed. His hand cupped her breast. Somehow in the night her bra had disappeared. 'That's better.'

'Warmer?'

'Yes, warmer.' Both his hands were occupied, taking up the heavy weight of her firm, full breasts. 'Nice,' she muttered. 'Sleepy.'

'Of course you are,' he said, sighing. The hands disappeared, to be replaced briefly by his warm, moist lips, teasing at each of her nipples. Beth squirmed with total enjoyment. And then the blankets came up and over her. She snuggled into the downy nest, smiled at him, and went back to sleep.

And so she missed the rest of the evening's entertainment. As Frank came out of her room, her dress and slip over one arm, another set of lights snapped on, illuminating the entire hall.

'And just what the hell is going on here?' Sue-Ann demanded.

'It's hard to explain,' he answered softly. 'Come out to the kitchen and I'll explain it all.'

'I'll just bet it's hard to explain,' Sue-Ann stated. 'Maybe I should call the police and let them listen?'

'No reason for that, Sue.'

'Sue-Ann is my name. This is my house. What the devil are you doing here at this hour of the night?'

'Boy,' he muttered. 'Maybe I was trying to steal your dog!'

'All you had to do is ask,' the blonde snapped. 'Those are Beth's things.'

'Come off it,' he said as he grabbed her arm and hustled her into the kitchen. 'Sit down.' It was a commanding voice; both girl and dog sat. 'Your sister was in a nasty accident,' he went on. 'I took her to the hospital, where they patched her up. But they gave her a shot to relax her muscles, and she fell asleep. So I brought her home.'

Sue-Ann required a minute or two to consider. Beautiful, he thought, with a brain about the size of a pea. Where did we go wrong, genetically speaking?

'And you put her to bed?'

'Well, somebody had to, and you weren't home.'

The blonde immediately went on to the defensive. 'I was only down in Slidell,' she said. 'There's a place——'

'I don't give a damn what place,' he said. 'We needed you and you weren't here, so I put your sister to bed.'

'You put—oh, gawd.' The girl shot up out of her chair and raced down the hall. The dog paced along behind her. In a minute she was back. 'Beth's in her bed,' she announced breathlessly, 'and she's naked!'

'I know that,' he growled. 'Will you get this stupid dog off my shoe? Didn't you feed the animal today?'

'No, I didn't feed the stupid animal today. I'm not the stupid animal feeder in this house. Beth's—naked. If she ever finds out that you—lordy, she'll go right through the roof, let me tell you!'

'I couldn't find a nightgown,' he protested. 'I was just trying my best to be neighbourly.'

'Oh? How was that?'

'She wanted to walk to prayer meeting. I couldn't let her walk alone, so I went along and——'

'You spent the whole evening with *my sister*?'

'Come on,' he said, shaking his head. 'Don't make a federal crime out of it.'

'And after I went to all that trouble to get a job at the Space Center, just to please you?'

'But I——'

'All you're going to get for your pains, *Mr* Wylie, is a hard time, just as soon as Beth finds out about—everything.' Sue-Ann was almost frothing at the mouth as she stamped up and down across the kitchen floor. 'All because you got the wrong sister!'

'What's that supposed to mean, Sue-Ann?'

'That's supposed to mean that if you wanted to undress a girl you could have found one more willing than Beth!'

'I see. And how is Beth going to find out?'

Those blue eyes speared him. The lovely little mouth twitched at one side, and a tear slid down Sue-Ann's face. 'I'm going to tell her, of course.'

And that, Frank Wylie told himself, is truly the end of the road. Little pea-brain here will shoot off her mouth, produce the wildest conclusions for Beth, and—I might as well move out of the neighbourhood. But before I go——

'Look, bird-brain,' he snapped. 'Your sister is pretty well knocked around. She's been ordered to stay in bed tomorrow. I'll be over a couple of times to check up. *You* are going to take care of her.'

'Me?'

'You. Close your mouth, you might catch flies. You're going to take care of her. And if you don't, little girl, you can just bet I'm going to put you over my knee and——'

'You can't talk to me like that!' Sue-Ann bellowed. Fang began to whine. There was too much emotion in the cake-mix tonight, and the dog couldn't handle it. Neither could Frank.

'Come on, dog,' he said. 'You'll come over to my pad for tonight. And as for you, Sue-Ann, you just remember what I've said.' He stood up, slamming his chair against the table for emphasis, and walked out into the hall. The dog followed him, nose to heel. Frank paused for a moment, thinking, and then walked down to Beth's room to check up on her.

She was still asleep, although half the blankets had fallen on the floor. In the shadowed light from the hall he knelt to restore her covers. Those magnificent breasts stood like unconquered hill forts, daring him. And Frank Wylie was not a man to be dared. Carefully, so as not to alarm her, he leaned over and kissed the peak of each ruddy hill again, and then pulled up the blankets, more to control himself than to keep her warm.

She stirred uneasily under the attention. He froze in position. She smiled in her sleep. 'Francis,' she said sleepily, and the smile deepened.

'Come on, mutt,' he whispered as he backed out the door. Fang followed along, grinning. The dog was finding this new game to be full of possibilities.

CHAPTER FIVE

By ELEVEN o'clock the next morning Beth Hendley was bored with life. She struggled out of bed, much surprised to find she was wearing no nightgown. Her foot, wrapped in half an acre of elastic bandage, ached. As did a fair proportion of the rest of her anatomy. The house was as quiet as a tomb.

She struggled down to the bathroom, filled the bath with equal parts of bubble bath and hot water, unwound her ungainly bandage and gave a tremendous sigh as she slipped into the comfort and warmth. Scented bubbles popped under her nose. Without thinking she pushed the remote control on the Sears agitator that turned her simple old bath into a whirlpool bath. The water circulated gently. She leaned back against the bath, adjusted the little air-pillow under her head, and began to consider the world.

He! In the beginning, there was he! Tall, broad, aggravating he! Francis Wylie. I wish I knew more about him, she thought. Where he comes from, who his family is, what his background is, why he's here. Her mother always maintained that if you wanted to know what your mate would be like twenty years down the road, look at his father today! But his father is dead, and his mother? Gone off? I wonder just what that means?

And what would he think of me? Small-town Baptist, whose biggest adventure was to go off to college. And then come right back home to teach in the high school where once I was a student. Three boyfriends. Count them—three. The first two were too young for me, and the last too old—and too fast with the fingers! Qualify all that. I went down to New Orleans for a week's vacation once. Remember? The French Quarter, seen through the eyes of a shy small-town girl? What a laugh he would have if he knew all that! Something tickled her nose. She brushed it away.

What is he doing here in Picayune? That had to be the first question, and she'd never learn anything by asking him. Therefore, Beth Hendley, you've got to get up out of your rut, put on your Sherlock Holmes hat, and find out.

Last night. At the risk of his own life he'd saved hers. Well, perhaps it wasn't all that dramatic, but you remember that big double-bumper coming at you like some dragon headed for dinner? So maybe he didn't save your life, but he came close enough to it to give him a gold star! And then after, when he carried you to the hospital emergency-room, remember? No mean feat, that. You're only five feet four, but you weigh more than a pound or two, girl. And he said words like 'love' and 'fiancée', and other delicious noises.

Of course they might all have been blarney. He was trying to wing his way past the doctor's orders, and you know that most men will say almost anything to get what they want!

What did he want? He was there every time I looked, holding my hand, and then the doctor stuck me with that needle and everything became very hazy. But *someone* brought me home. *Someone* held me close. I swear *someone* kissed me—lordy, kissed me in the most elegant places! And then Sukey must have put me to bed. Only I don't remember *that* part at all.

Something brushed over her nose. She scratched, but it wouldn't go away. Cautiously she opened one eye. A great mass of white cotton-candy bubbles towered above her head, reaching a third of the way to the ceiling. 'Great gobs of goose grease,' she muttered.

'Are you going to eat it or wear it?' the deep bass voice behind her asked. She surged up and looked over her shoulder, and then promptly sank to chin-level.

'What are you doing here?'

'It's lunchtime. I thought to come and check on the invalid.'

'I mean—what are you doing in my bathroom?' So it sounds as if I'm angry, she told herself. Mainly because I am!

He seemed to think that the question was superfluous. He leaned over the bath, stabbed a bit of the white concoction on his finger, and tasted it. 'Good lord. Soap!'

'What did you expect? Of course it's soap. Out. Out!'

'I could be a big help. Want me to wash your back?'

'What I want,' she said very slowly, trying to sound each syllable distinctly, 'is for you to go away.'

'You don't have to be so hard to get along with,' he said morosely. 'I can't see a thing except for your nose. What happened?'

'What do you suppose?' she asked firmly, and then, because the truth was her normal intercourse, 'I put too much bubble bath in, and then forgot about it. The agitator has made a mountain out of it. Out!'

'OK. I'll go make us some lunch. Are you sure you can get out?' She wasn't all that sure, but had no intention of telling him so. Her glare pushed him back a step or two.

'I can get out,' she muttered. 'So can you. Close the door after you.'

'Spoilsport!'

It wasn't quite the ladylike thing to do, but she stuck her tongue out at him. He was laughing as he walked out.

Her toe fished around for the button that drained the bath. The water ran out, but the mound of soap didn't. She turned over on hands and knees, managed to slide over the edge of the bath, and ended up on the mat, still sticky with chunks of soap cloud. And the door came open.

'I heard the noise,' he said anxiously. 'Hurt yourself?'

'No, darn it,' she growled. 'I always lie on the floor after my bath. Will you get out of here?'

'No need to be snooty about it,' he grumbled. And then grinned. 'Your bubbles are popping.'

'Out!' she roared as she struggled to her feet. Her hand found the only weapon available. He winked at her as he saw her palm the plastic bottle of bubble bath, and ducked behind the door. The bottle travelled a good thousand miles in the wrong direction, but his laughter haunted her as she scraped off the soap, dried herself with the rough bath-towel, slipped into her ancient green robe, and reapplied her bandage.

He was in the kitchen, hard at work, when she limped out. 'Club sandwiches,' he squeezed in before she could work up a good bellow. 'Ham and roast beef. I know you like it.'

'I—how did you know that?'

'Because you're a roast beef girl,' he said, chuckling. 'Just look at you. All red and rosy. And if you wore your hair that way at school we'd have to arrest you for maintaining an Attractive Nuisance. Here, let me.'

He came around the table with a silly grin on his face. She backed off a barefoot step or two, trembling. His hands reached out towards her. She retreated another step. The hands went to the tie of her robe, pulled it tighter, tucked in the folding edge, and retied the knot. Why am I trembling like this? she asked herself. He's not going to rape and pillage during the lunch hour, is he? And Sue-Ann is——

'Where's my sister?' she asked.

'You wouldn't believe.'

'I'm willing to believe anything at this point,' she said, exasperated.

'Beth, your sister is next door at my house. She said something silly about vacuuming under the beds. Who am I to restrain great endeavours? About the sandwiches?'

'I love club sandwiches,' she admitted, surrendering. 'With an olive on the top?'

He held out a chair for her, and ushered her gallantly into it. 'With an onion as well if you want it.' He dropped into the chair opposite her. 'Your sister. Does she have all her marbles?'

'Of course she does,' Beth answered indignantly. 'She's a sweet, lovable girl. Beautiful, too. And has lots of money.' A pause for further reflection. 'Sue-Ann is a sort of primitive,' she mused. 'When she sees what she wants she grabs it. People who get in her way, or cross her, can get hurt.'

'Great,' he muttered from around a huge bite of sandwich. 'Just the kind of girl that any man would want, I suppose?'

'You'd better believe it.' A pause while she gently masticated a tiny bite, her small white teeth flashing at him. 'There's lots of competition too where Sue-Ann is concerned. If you intend to play in her league you'd better get your bid in early.' And then, to be perfectly honest, 'Of course she's a little young. But she has me to look after her!'

'Do I hear a little threat there?'

'You do, Mr Wylie.'

'You don't have to threaten me for your sister's sake, Miss Hendley.' He was staring at her from across the table, the tip of his nose twitching as she bit into her sandwich. What are you having for lunch? he asked himself as he squirmed in his chair. Beth Hendley on toast?

'I'm glad to hear my sister isn't at risk,' she answered firmly. 'You make a delicious sandwich—and I thank you.'

'Well, don't get your hopes set too high,' he said gruffly. 'Maybe it's *your* pretty white body I'm after!' And along with that went his famous imitation of a Groucho Marx leer.

'Well, really—Mr Wylie!' She had taken one swallow too many, and almost choked.

'Why, after all I was to you last night, is it still *Mr Wylie*?'

She sipped at her glass of milk, and managed to keep from expiring on the spot. 'In the bright light of day things have a different perspective, Mr Wylie. Did you handle my classes this morning?'

And how is that for a quick change of subject? he asked himself. This girl has more wiggles than a worm on the hook. But if she doesn't intend to play, I'll have to go along with her. A lock of his crisp black hair had fallen down over his forehead. He brushed it away. 'Now that's a story worth considering. I took your first class before the social studies department rescued me. What happened to the old "memorise the textbook" routine?'

'We don't do things that way any more, sir.'

'That does it. I could put up with "Mr Wylie", but *sir*—that's going a step too far.' He started to get up from the table.

Good lord, Beth told herself as he towered over her.
What in the world am I doing? We're all alone in my
kitchen, I'm wearing practically nothing, and he has the
look of an enraged bear! Babble, she told herself as she
shrank back into her chair.

'It's a project approach that we use. We want the
students to get into the library, to think about what's
presented. As with the little girl on the hand-out. You
did give them the hand-out?' Am I babbling too fast?
I can't seem to help it. I'm out of breath!

'You mean the story about the bones of the little girl?'

'Yes. The one discovered by archaeologists in a cave
up the Neander River in Germany.'

'Yes, I gave them the paper. I don't know when I've
heard a bigger groan.'

She grinned up at him, her courage restored. 'It's that
way whenever you call on them to think. By the time
they're delivered to us, all they're accustomed to is having
facts shovelled down their throats. At the high-school
level we're trying to lead them to learn how to *use* an
encyclopaedia, not how to *be* one! But it doesn't take
them long to discover that problem-solving is a game.'

'And just what are they supposed to discover from
this poor little girl?'

'Oh, a great deal. Like Neander—Neanderthal man.
Somebody loved the child or they wouldn't have buried
her. Somebody placed a bowl of wild millet at her feet
so they anticipated an after-life. The beads under her
neck were amber—which means not only did they
appreciate a little adornment, but since amber could only
be found in those days on the shores of the Baltic, they
had a trade going. She was buried in the foetal position.
Is that just an accident, or did Neanderthal man know
more than we think he did about anatomy? There are
dozens of things, if only we can prod the kids to stop

and consider them. We call the programme Inferences. It runs for two weeks, after which they'll know everything there is to know about prehistoric man.'

'Good lord! And, if you're lucky, restore some of that curiosity that young people are born with?'

'That's better.'

'What's better?'

She offered him a sunny smile again. 'You didn't curse.'

'Well I'll be d—darned!'

'So you will.'

He settled back in his chair, tapping an impatient finger on the table. One leg of the table was too short; every time he banged that huge finger down, everything rocked. She took a good look at him. Something was going on behind that forehead of his. Those dark eyes were unfocused, as if he were seeing through time instead of space. A big bear of a man, she told herself. Could someone like me—tame him? Maybe that was the wrong word. Coexist safely with him? Her mother's dry voice came back through memory. 'You marry the man who is, not who you'd like him to be. No amount of striving can change a man *after* he marries.' But then, how did *marriage* get into the conversation?

'Last night, at the hospital...' Her voice wavered. She brushed her hair back with a nervous hand.

'Yes?' he prodded.

'You said—you told the doctor that I was—your fiancée. Why did you do that?'

'Did I say that?' The astonished sound in his voice was just perfect, but there was a twinkle in his eyes.

'You know you did,' she answered indignantly.

'If you say so, I must have,' he replied. 'Maybe it was the shock?'

'You've got that mixed up. *I* was the one in shock, not you.'

'Ah, but sometimes that's catching.' He leaned back in his chair and fingered his necktie. 'I've seen that happen dozens of times. You know, they snap the ball, and the guy next to you gets knocked on his—on his back—and you immediately feel a reaction.'

'What kind of a reaction?' she snapped.

'Fear,' he replied instantly. 'Inordinate amounts of fear.' She started to file a rebuttal, but he held up his hand in a stop signal. 'Now tell me,' he rumbled, 'what the name of that driver was. He was a student, wasn't he?'

'I haven't any idea what you're talking about,' she protested, crossing her fingers behind her back.

'Last night,' he said patiently. 'The truck that tried to run you down. Who was the driver?'

'I—haven't the vaguest idea. The headlights were in my eyes. I couldn't see beans. I told you that.'

'And you a woman of the Church,' he growled. 'You know there are sins of omission as well as sins of commission.'

Indignation was her only defence. She fell back on it with vim. 'You'd be the one to know about sins! I'll bet there aren't many you've not experienced! What a colossal nerve you have, Mr Wylie!'

'So we agree on that.' He scraped back his chair and stood up, glaring down at her. 'I don't know when I've met a more obstinate woman. If I had time I'd get the truth out of you, but I haven't. I'll stop by after school. Where is that prescription the doctor gave you for pain?'

'I—don't remember.' And this time it was the absolute truth.

'Ah,' he muttered, fishing in his own pockets. 'I've got it. I'll go and get it filled—where the devil is there a pharmacy?'

'You don't know a thing about Picayune, do you?' she challenged. 'Whatever brought you here?'

'You?' he asked mischievously. 'Now, the drug store?'

'Westside Pharmacy,' she snapped, aggravated for some reason she didn't understand. 'On the other side of the hospital, on Kirkwood Street. I have an account there.'

'I suppose I could find it.' That big grin was back again.

'Don't let me put you out of your way.' She straggled to her feet as well, clutching at the knot in her belt for modesty's sake.

'Lord, I don't understand you,' he muttered as he headed for the door. 'One minute you're sweet enough to eat, and the next you spit like an angry cat. Good day!'

And good day to you, she told herself sadly as she watched him stomp down the porch steps and head for the school. I don't understand me either. I wish you didn't have to go. I wish I could be all sweetness and love. I wish—but there are always so many 'why's and 'what's and unanswered 'when's—am I really lying to him all that much? And besides, there's still and always Sue-Ann.

She struggled down the hall to her own room. Her foot felt considerably improved; the bruises—well, they ached, but not too badly. It didn't seem worthwhile to dress. She lay back on the bed and pulled a light sheet up over her. And it was only as her head hit the pillow that she realised. He had dodged and twisted and turned, and *never* answered her question about why he'd called her his fiancée!

*   *   *

It had been a hard afternoon. The telephone-absentee system had bugs to be worked out. There were a certain number of disciplinary problems that fell to his lot because, honorary or otherwise, he was the assistant principal. There had been a warm glow arising from his meeting after school with all the athletic coaches. 'Look,' he had finally summarised, 'there's no simple solution to our problem, getting more of our young people to stay in school and do better. I have about twenty-five items we're going to try out in this first semester. But this is one for you. The kids all feel a closer affinity to a school that provides extra-curricular activities. And kids seldom drop out if they're involved in those activities. The thing that turns them on fastest is a successful athletic programme. So whatever you do, from football to tiddly-winks, do it thoroughly, and do it with good sportsmanship. And I'm not knocking the desire to win! Now you'll have to excuse me. I've got to get over to the drama club and give them the same pitch!'

Ms Margaret met him in the hall as he headed for home. Besides themselves, only the janitors were still at work. 'Long day,' the principal commented. He could see that she was as tired as he.

'For everybody,' he acknowledged. 'But there's always hope. Do I dare to say there's light at the end of the tunnel?'

She laughed at him as he held the door for her. 'I can see you're not from around these parts. We're flat land in all directions. I don't suppose you'll find a tunnel anywhere this side of New Orleans. But yes, I have the feeling that we may do a little better this year. And that's our goal, isn't it? Do a little better, year by year?'

The idea plagued him as he walked down Third Avenue. Just do a little better. But can I live long enough to make it all the way with Beth Hendley? He shrugged

GALORE

There's no cost— and no obligation to buy anything!

We'd like to send you free gifts to introduce you to the benefits of the Harlequin Reader Service®: free home delivery of brand-new Harlequin Romance® novels months before they're available in stores, and at a savings from the cover price!

Accepting our free gifts places you under no obligation to buy anything ever. You may cancel the Reader Service at any time, even just after receiving your free gifts, simply by writing "cancel" on your statement or returning a shipment of books to us at our cost. But if you choose not to cancel, every month we'll send you six more Harlequin Romance® novels, and bill you just $2.47* apiece—and there's **no** extra charge for shipping and handling. There are **no** hidden extras!

PEEK-A-BOO!

Free Gifts For You!

Look inside—Right Now!
We've got something
special just for you!

his shoulders. Somehow his long, formal education had failed him in a very important subject.

He stopped by his own house for a quick shower and a change into something less formal. The Cablevision company had come to install his little black box. He carelessly flicked through the thirty-one channels, and turned it off. Out in his extensive back garden the grass was higher than ever, but he didn't own a lawnmower. Maybe if I decide to stay in Picayune longer, he thought, we could put a swimming-pool right there in the middle. *We?* He chuckled at his own temerity.

So some progress had been made. He shoved his hands deep into his pockets and wondered why he was fidgeting so much. Nervousness was not a trait from which he normally suffered. The Ice Man, they had called him back in Atlanta, because he had always kept his cool, no matter what the provocation. And it had paid off. After his first season as a professional football player he had dumped the groupies and the wild parties, invested all his spare time searching for his advanced degrees at the University of Georgia, and had taken over active guidance of his own investments. Nine long years, almost celibate. And out of touch with the female mind.

Sukey, for example. A beautiful girl with a glass character, ready to crack under any strain. And Beth loved her. Obvious choice, man. If you want Beth, you have to learn to treat Sukey with kid gloves!

Light flashed through the thick privet hedge. So look at that, he lectured himself. You're standing here trying to find more reasons why you shouldn't rush next door and see how—and see. So go, idiot!

It shouldn't be said that he *ran* down the length of the hedge and up the other side, but he certainly walked with a full head of steam. Somebody was rocking in the swing on the veranda, but it was still light enough to see that it was the wrong somebody.

'Sue-Ann,' he acknowledged gravely.

'Frank. How nice of you to come by. Just back from school?'

'Just back.' She patted the space beside her. He sat down gingerly. The old canvas swing was not quite prepared for him. It sagged and groaned. Sue-Ann giggled.

'It's not because you're so heavy,' she said, 'it's because it's so old. Did you have a bad day?'

'Middling-fair,' he reported. 'And you? How did your job go?'

'Job? Oh, lord, Frank. That was a terrible mistake. I'm not cut out to be a tour guide. Did you like the way I cleaned your house?'

'I—yes,' he said, although he hadn't noticed at all. The swing had sagged down on his side, and the girl was sliding down the incline, by gravity or by purpose. He could feel the warmth of her thigh as it came in contact with his. There were no inches on his other side to which he might retreat. She wasn't the girl he wanted. Whatever he did would probably be wrong—and get him further into Beth's black book! He offered Sukey a very chaste, very brotherly kiss on her forehead.

'Thanks for the house-cleaning. I came by to see how Beth is making out.'

'Oh, pooh. Beth's doing fine. Why don't you kiss me?'

Yeah, why don't I? he asked himself. Commit suicide, why don't you? Kiss the little girl and then listen as glass breaks and tinkles all around you. Sue-Ann had come up on her knees and leaned over him, brooding. The sweet smell, the softness, the warmth were all there, but not the temptation.

'Sukey,' he said quietly, 'you're the loveliest girl I've seen in years. But you're twenty years old, and I'm thirty-six. When you're as old as thirty, I'll be forty-six. Over the hill. I'm not for you, love.'

But Sue-Ann was not to be deterred. She leaned closer, and kissed him gently on the lips. He could feel her quivering, but for him it was like eating an ice-cream bar. Plenty of sweetness, but enough cold to turn off his engine.

'Wasn't that wonderful?' she asked coyly, moments later.

'I've got to see Beth,' he muttered, and got up. Sukey watched him. Lord knows what she's thinking, he told himself. Her lips are parted, and she's breathing heavily. She looked like a woman sure of her prey, and all he could do was run away.

'I'm tired,' he complained as he took a step or two away. 'Let's just take a rain-check. I brought this prescription and I want to see how Beth goes on, and then I think I'll hit the sack.'

'What's the matter, Frank? Too tired? Got a headache? I thought that was *my* line.'

'Sue-Ann,' he warned. In the gathering darkness he could see her teeth gleam, as if she were ready to bite.

'Yes, as you say, a rain-check.' She put out her hand and he helped her up. They were still holding hands as they went into the house. Beth was sitting in the kitchen, her foot up, playing with her dog. Fang—Pansy—skidded across the floor to welcome Frank, jumping up at him, wagging the whole body and not just the tail.

'Beth,' he acknowledged.

'Mr Wylie.'

'I wanted to see how you were feeling.' There was no way to control the dog, except to pick him up. When he did, Fang scrubbed his face with a rough tongue.

'Yes, I could see that you did.' Beth Hendley was doing her best to contain herself, but portions of her anguish were leaking out on all sides. Her sharp eye could hardly have missed her sister's hand in his, nor could her sharp mind leave it alone. Surely he came to see me, she thought. Of course he did. That's why Sue-Ann is looking at him with angelic guilt. You bet, Mr Wylie, how good of you to come to check on my health.

'So I'm still wondering.' There was a hint of laughter in his voice, which made Beth angrier than before. But a hard Baptist conscience locked her in—and besides, there was nothing to throw at him but her best china. Her mother's best china. And that she would not sacrifice for *any* man.

'You needn't worry,' she said coldly. 'I'm well enough to come in to work tomorrow.'

'That's not what I meant.' His face grew red with anger, but Beth was too wrapped up in her own hurts to notice. And Sue-Ann, watching them both, saw a perfect opportunity to nip in the bud what she considered to be a dangerous liaison.

'Oh, you two mustn't fight,' she said cheerily. 'After all, I gather that you had a marvellous adventure last night. Just the two of you!' There was the vibrant sound of anger behind the last sentence.

'I wouldn't exactly call it an adventure,' Frank Wylie said. 'You heard something about it?'

'Oh, a little something,' Sue-Ann responded. 'That police sergeant came around while you were asleep this afternoon, Beth. He wanted to ask some more questions. Somebody actually tried to run you down, that's what he said. And you were hurt?'

'Something like that,' Beth answered softly. 'It wasn't all that important. Just a silly accident. I might have slipped, or the driver might have lost control. Anyway, Frank—Mr Wylie, grabbed me out of the way, and that's about all.'

'About all?' Sue-Ann's laugh was a little more shrill than usual. Frank flinched, as if the sound was grating on him. 'About all,' Sue-Ann repeated. 'And then he drove you home and carried you in the house, I suppose. And then stripped you naked and put you to bed. Oh, I *do* hope that's all he did!'

'But—Sue-Ann. I thought that you——'

'Me?' That shrill laugh again, cutting through the silent room like a sharp knife through cake. 'Not me, sister. I didn't get home until Frankie boy was on his way home. And now I'm sure you two have things to talk about. I'm going straight to bed. Don't forget, Frank. Rain-checks!' At which the willowy blonde swayed out of the room, giggling to herself.

Even the dog felt oppressed by the silence in the kitchen. By now Frank Wylie had put him down on the floor. The animal slunk off into a corner, so dejected that his stomach was dragging on the floor.

Beth had already gone through the cycle of emotion. Fear, anger, rage, and now despondency. She leaned both elbows on the table and supported her chin with cupped hands. Her body was not responding well to command, and her brain felt heavy, almost useless. 'I—suppose what she said was true?' Spoken quietly, almost like a librarian having a conference in the reading-room.

'Not exactly.' He shrugged his shoulders and sighed. There was no way in the world to avoid the problem.

'What part, exactly, wasn't true? You did carry me into the house?'

'Yes, that's true.'

'And you did—put me to bed?' A little quaver tugged at the corner of her mouth.

'Yes, I did that.'

'And you—took off all my clothes?'

'Yes, I did that.'

'Then what part of what Sue-Ann said could be untrue? Are you telling me that you—you didn't do another single thing beyond that?'

'No, I'm not telling you that, Beth. You have a marvellous body. I was attracted. But I did *not* do what Sue was implying—and what you think I did!'

She lifted her head. He could see tears in her eyes, but her face was fashioned in a Madonna look that could not be deciphered. 'Then I suppose I have that to thank you for, Mr Wylie?'

'You don't have anything to thank me for,' he replied. 'And I have a lot on my conscience, Beth Hendley. I don't know what the custom is down here in Mississippi, but I think we ought to announce our engagement tomorrow.'

Her head snapped up. 'Engagement to what?' she shot back at him. 'Me be engaged to you? Do you think I'd marry a—person like you, Frank Wylie? Damn you!'

'Uh-uh,' he teased. 'We mustn't curse, love.'

'Yes,' she snapped. 'You've finally got me falling to your level. Well, the answer is still no.'

'I'm said to be a good catch,' he commented. 'I've got my health, and a reasonable bank account, and——'

'And a glib tongue,' she interjected. 'I knew it from the first minute that I saw you. Carpetbagger!'

'I guess that about concludes the evening,' he said. 'And I have your little sister and her loose tongue to blame it all. Can I help you to bed?'

Beth jumped to her feet, swaying. 'Not on your everloving life!' she yelled at him. 'Wasn't once enough?'

'I—I didn't mean anything like that,' he came back at her. 'You are about the most opinionated, stubborn, mule-headed woman I've ever known. Look out!'

Beth, in her anger, had started across the floor, bumped her damaged foot on the leg of a chair, and was halfway to the floor, crying, when he caught her and swept her up in his arms.

'Put me down, you—you philanderer,' she managed through the tears.

'When I'm damn good and ready,' he announced bitterly.

'I——'

'Shut up. Just shut up,' he muttered as he marched down the hall and into her bedroom. The bed was unmade. He sat her down in the chair at the head of the bed and proceeded to straighten everything out. Beth, sitting dejectedly in the chair, could not allow him to escape a parting shot.

'You've had a lot of practice making up women's beds.'

'You'd better believe it,' he muttered as he came back around the bed and swept her up out of the chair. Why tell her that one of his jobs had been as a nursing aide while he'd worked his way through undergraduate school? She could almost feel the heat of his anger. But he stretched her out gently on the bed, and then bent to look at her bandaged ankle. 'Are you *sure* about this? I don't think you ought to come to work tomorrow.'

'I'll come if I have to call on the devil for help,' she snarled.

'Well, do that,' he returned angrily. 'Just call. I'll be available!' He pulled the sheet up over her, tucking it in gently around her chin, and then bent over her.

'Don't do that,' she squeaked.

'Shut up,' he muttered, and kissed her gently. There was no great fire in this meeting. It was a comforting kiss, one that left her with an empty feeling. He set a prescription bottle down on her bedside table and stalked

out the door. She snatched up the bottle as if to throw
it after him, but her eye caught the label. 'Take two for
pain,' it said, and oh, lord, she knew full well that
nothing in a bottle could help her with the pain in her
heart.

Sukey peeped into the bedroom after Frank had gone.
Beth managed a weak smile. 'He's a strong, dominant
man,' she suggested.

'And good-looking,' her stepsister said as she wrapped
her arms around herself. 'I want him.'

It wasn't exactly late. A low quarter-moon pranced across
the black sky. Town lights obscured some of the stars,
but it was not like being in a big city. The trees screened
out many of the constellations, but there were enough
to enjoy. And, more than one might expect, the citizens
of Picayune were interested in the stars and planets,
which were waiting out there for space vehicles propelled
by engines whose last testings were at the Stennis Space
Center, where the majority of the town's citizens were
employed.

So Frank Wylie paused on the front steps of his own
house, counted stars, and made a belated 'star-bright'
wish of his own. The soft breeze of autumn plucked at
his shirt. He could feel a cool spot or two where Beth's
tears had dampened him, and where the wind was
working its evaporative wonder. 'Damn,' he muttered,
and went into the house.

His kitchen, he noticed for the first time, was almost
identical to the one next door, but considerably less neat.
The idea bothered him. He kicked a chair out of his way
and went to the refrigerator for a beer. And then, not
too many minutes later, for another.

'Sit down and go over your plans for the week,' he
ordered. The sitting was easy, but the concentrating was

impossible. Disgusted with himself, he went into the bathroom, shedding clothing on the way. His Aunt Harriet always hated that habit of his; Beth would too, he told himself grimly. But you've so thoroughly screwed things up, you and that pea-brained sister of hers, that there sure as hell isn't going to be any happy ever after, is there, stupid?

When he stepped into the shower the cold water surprised him. Normally he would have reached for the hot tap. Tonight it just didn't seem to matter. He danced a little bit to keep his teeth from chattering, and then bounded out on to the rug. The towel had been hanging on a hot rail. He accepted the pleasure of it as he rubbed himself dry in front of the mirror.

You're not really falling apart, he told himself. Everybody gets scars playing professional football. So you're over thirty-five. You've still got a massive set of deltoids. Broad shoulders, narrow waist. Well, not as narrow as once it was. There's a little roll of fat there at belly-level. Maybe you should work that off, Tarzan? Somebody like Beth would never want to put up with some guy sporting a beer-gut!

And if she likes a man with hair on his chest, lord, you've got enough for yourself and two other guys. A damn bear, like your father. He barely brushed down his mop of hair, and struggled off to bed still damp on top.

There were no lights on in the bedroom, and the shades were pulled down. He never wore pyjamas. He was a violent sleeper, rolling from side to side, curling and stretching madly. When he *did* try to put on the class he always found himself twisted up in the pyjama jackets, almost throttling himself. So for tonight, naked as he was born, still a little damp, he slid into the massive bed that his size and weight required.

And found it already occupied.

Sue-Ann Foster, inhabiting a thin cotton shorty nightgown, had evidently had to wait too long to collect on her rain-check, and was fast asleep in his bed, hugging a pillow to her as if it were a precious doll. Frank Wylie groaned.

CHAPTER SIX

For a moment Frank Wylie lay there in bed as if paralysed. It had been a long, long time since a voluptuous young woman had wanted to share his bed, and this one meant trouble. With a capital 'T'. First of all, she was the sister of a certain lady whose friendship he wanted very badly. Second, he was an assistant principal in a small-town school, where a single word of scandal would bring an end to all his experiments. Third, the girl in the bed had a tongue that was hinged in the middle so it could wiggle at both ends, and not enough brains to get off the tracks when the train was coming!

Carefully, moving an inch at a time, he eased himself out of the bed and down on to the floor. Sue-Ann stirred, muttered something indistinguishable, and rolled over on her side, facing away from him. Hold your breath, he ordered himself. One false move and she's going to start raising hell or playing wedding bells! Flat on his stomach he wriggled his way to the bedroom door, and out into the hall, where he stood and closed the bedroom door. What to do? His hands were somewhat more efficient than his brain.

He found a pair of dungarees and slipped into them. His shoes had disappeared in the night, and he dared not put on a light. More fumbling discovered a shirt, with the sleeves so entangled that he could not get it on. And the only thing his brain came up with was 'get Beth'. Which hardly made any sense at all. Nevertheless he went out into the darkness, cut his bare toe on the shovel he

had carelessly discarded by the rose-bed, and hobbled
up on to the porch of the house next door.

Beth Hendley heard the noise, but decided to ignore it.
The dream into which she had fallen had become very
exotic—or was the correct word erotic? In any event,
she wriggled further down under the covers and tried to
woo her way back into the fantasy. Without success.
Someone was hammering on the front door with a pick-
axe. Or so it seemed. Fang, hiding under the bed, came
out cautiously, growling.

‘Get ’em, Pansy,’ she coaxed. The dog growled again,
and refused to move. Beth rubbed her eyes with one bare
hand, and swung her legs out of the bed. ‘Get ’em,
Fang!’ Her little dog yipped, and bolted down the hall,
where presently, from in front of the front door, he set
up a maddening howl.

‘Oh, brother,’ Beth moaned feebly as she reached for
her alarm clock. Two in the morning. She moaned again
as she grappled around on the floor for her slippers. The
pounding continued; the dog yapped as if he were eager
to assault a burglar. Completely out of patience, Beth
managed to hobble down the hall, using one hand to
trail along the wall and keep her upright. She was still
half asleep, but anger was nibbling at the edges of her
consciousness. There was a rush mat on the floor in front
of the door. Naturally she tripped over it, and bumped
her head on the door-frame. ‘At times,’ she whispered
to herself, ‘it becomes very difficult to be a Christian.’
Whoever was banging on the door continued.

‘Cut that out!’ she yelled. Another couple of massive
bangs shook the solid oak door. The latch slipped and
the door swung inward. ‘It wasn’t even locked,’ she
protested bitterly. ‘Who—what? Dear lord in heaven!’

The pair of them stood and stared at each other. He outside the door, dressed only in his dungarees, shivering in the night wind; she, inside, enveloped in her thin lawn nightgown, covered from neck to ankle in gossamer transparency, her mouth half open. Her dog was across the threshold, licking Frank Wylie's bare toe. 'Traitor,' she muttered.

'He likes me,' Frank retorted.

'I know that,' she snapped. 'But he's only a dumb animal. Is my house on fire?'

'Fire? I didn't see—oh, no, your house isn't on fire. I wish I could say mine was.'

Beth had finally recognised the sparsity of her clothing. She hugged herself, but curiosity drove her. She stepped out on the porch beside him, and looked over the hedge as his place. No glow lit the sky. 'Your house isn't on fire either,' she stated flatly.

'I know that,' he growled. 'What a stupid conversation this is——'

'At this hour of the day,' she interrupted sharply, 'what would you expect? Ben Jonson?'

'What I would expect,' he grumbled, 'is that any sane woman would invite me in so we could discuss the problem without benefit of the neighbours.'

'I think you've got it all wrong, Mr Wylie. Any woman who would let you into her house at two in the morning, and you barely wearing a pair of pants, would be far from sane. What is your problem?'

And if that isn't cold enough, she told herself, I'll put a little more ice in it. After all, he's only the assistant principal from eight in the morning to four-thirty in the afternoon. The nerve of the man, flaunting his bare chest at me as if we were on the beach. What tremendous shoulders he has! Those pants are barely being held up. They sag down around his hips and——

'Sue-Ann,' he snapped.

The name spun her around, mentally speaking. Two o'clock in the morning, and the code-word is Sue-Ann? Great Day In The Morning! 'Come in, Mr Wylie,' she gasped. 'Quickly!'

He ghosted by her, her dog followed, and Beth quickly closed the front door behind her and leaned against it. 'What about Sue-Ann?' she muttered defiantly.

'Your idiot sister, Miss Hendley, is next door in my bed, fast asleep, that's what about!'

'What?'

'Don't "what" me, lady. That idiot sister of yours is——'

'Now just a darn minute, Mr Wylie! If my sister is in your bed it's only because you seduced her into it. I told you you'd have me to account to, damn you!'

'Uh-uh, we mustn't curse!'

'I'll curse and scream and run you up one side and down the other, you...'

'Arrogant?'

'That's *one* of the words that apply. Arrant, arrogant, supercilious, over-sexed——'

'Hey, I like that one,' he interrupted as he grabbed her arm. 'Now for once in your life sit down and listen!' She had little choice. There was only one chair in the front hall, a fragile 1890s round chair with a padded seat. He plumped her down on to it with little regard for its ancient legs.

'What—what are you doing?' It was a question she had to ask, but one whose answer she didn't want to know. If he had intended to frighten her, to intimidate her, he had managed quite well. She shivered visibly.

'Dear lord,' he shouted at her, 'I'm not going to eat you!' And then, more softly, gentler, 'I don't mean to frighten you, Beth.'

She dabbed at her eyes with the sleeve of her nightgown. 'For someone who didn't mean to, you've succeeded remarkably well. What have you done to my sister?'

He pulled her back up to her feet, and cursed under his breath as he saw her wince. 'Your foot still hurts?'

'It didn't before you came pounding on my door.' She couldn't hide the gusty sigh that put a stop to the tears. He tilted her head up with one finger under her chin.

'I can't seem to win, can I? Everything I touch turns to sh...sugar. Look, love, I didn't mean any of this to happen. When your sister started playing domestic in my house I thought it was one of those queer little ideas of hers that were bound to pass sooner or later. And now she's in the middle of my bed; I swear to you on a stack of bibles I haven't seduced the girl, I don't plan to do so in the immediate future, but if she wakes up tomorrow morning under my roof there'll be hell to pay in Picayune. What do we do next?'

'We?' It seemed appropriate for a tired girl with a bad foot to lean forward and rest her head in the middle of all those dark curls on his chest. A very comfortable nest, her conscience reported. Very comfortable indeed. And *he* didn't seem to mind in the least. Except that he seemed to be breathing at a faster pace than before. 'We?' she repeated. 'Now all of a sudden it's a conspiracy?'

'Give me strength,' he muttered into her own curls. Her head fitted very neatly under his chin. Some of her hair must be bothering him, for he kept running his free hand through its silky strands. 'I'm not trying to implicate you in a crime,' he said softly. His lips were right at her ear. Along with the words she felt the warmth of his breath, a tingling, sparkling warmth. 'But I do need help to get out of this mess, love.'

And there it was again. *Love.* Maybe that was something they said all the time up in Baltimore? She hoped not. 'You couldn't carry her back over here, I don't suppose?'

'Oh, I could carry her all right, but not without waking her up.'

'Just suppose,' Beth mused, and then paused for a moment. 'Just suppose when Sue-Ann wakes up we're *all* under your roof. We had a—a pipe burst in the kitchen. How's that?'

'Beth, what a wonderful idea. Great. I'll carry you over. We won't have to worry about waking *you* up. And we can bring the dog as well, and——'

Beth lost the rest of the words. He was a man of action, no doubt about that. He thrust open the front door, swung Beth up in his arms, whistled for the dog, and started out into the night. She buried her face against his shoulder. It was already too late to say something about 'Not dressed in just my nightgown you won't'. Or, 'Who's going to turn me off after riding all that distance so close to you?' Or, 'I really don't like you, Mr Wylie—Francis'. Or, 'Suppose someone sees us?'

None of that was pertinent, anyway. When he managed to get to the pavement, and was about to turn up into his driveway, a spotlight silhouetted the pair of them, and a distinctly police voice said, 'All right, just stop right there!'

'Oh, hell,' Frank muttered.

'I believe that's just what I would have said,' Beth added glumly.

'Just stand right where you are,' the young patrolman said. Beth, peering over Frank's shoulder, could see the flashlight shaking, and the drawn gun in the other hand.

'Yes,' she said submissively, and pounded her fist on Frank's cheek when it looked as if he had other ideas.

'Show me some identification.'

'Can I put the lady down?'

'But carefully.' The pistol gestured. 'Don't make a false move.'

'No, I wouldn't think of it,' Frank said, sighing. 'Watch a lot of *Miami Vice* on television, do you?'

'No conversation. Identification. You, lady!'

'I—just don't normally carry identification in my nightgown,' Beth offered tentatively.

'And I don't have a thing either,' Frank added. 'I guess you'll have to take us down to the station.'

'Frank!' Beth twisted away from his arm, which was still on her shoulder. 'What are you saying?'

'Well, when you're right you're right,' Frank Wylie said in his most incautious tone. 'The officer is right. Are you arresting us?'

'There've been a lot of prowler complaints in this neighbourhood,' the patrolman replied. 'I guess——'

'Don't,' a second voice behind them interrupted. Sergeant Matthews stepped into the light. The same sergeant who had interviewed them at the hospital. The same sergeant who was one of the senior wardens at the First Baptist Church. The same sergeant who——

'Ms Beth,' the older man acknowledged. 'Out for a stroll? And Dr Wylie, I believe?'

'Stanley and Liverwurst,' Frank Wylie muttered angrily.

'*Livingstone*,' Beth corrected. 'Stanley and Livingstone. Good evening, Sergeant. How is Mrs Matthews today?'

'Home in bed, like most good people of this town. Not dressed for strolling, either one of you, are you?'

'You could say that,' Frank agreed. 'There was this emergency, and——'

'That's not what we called it in my day,' the sergeant interrupted. And then he turned to the younger patrolman. 'Well, don't stand there gawking. Get back to the car!' The patrolman slunk away.

'And as for you two,' the church warden said, 'you'd better give some serious thought to getting married.' With which philosophical comment he disappeared into the darkness. A moment later the patrol-car lights came on, and moved smartly up Third Avenue in the direction of the Arboretum.

Beth, who had been holding her breath for what seemed like hours, let it all run out. 'Good lord,' she exclaimed as she moved closer to Frank—for the shared warmth, she told herself. Full of the same idea, he put an arm around her shoulders and hugged her.

'Don't worry,' he chided. 'They're not making a report of it.'

'Not to the police department,' she replied bitterly. 'He's an elder of the church.'

'Maybe I can get a post in Antarctica,' he commented.

Beth allowed herself to be swayed by the warmth, by the comfort, but only for a moment. Then she pushed herself away. 'By this time next week my reputation is going to be mud,' she said.

'Or maybe you'll be married. In which case the mud will all wash off.'

'Fat chance,' she raged. 'Willy Norton is the only eligible in the area, and I couldn't bring him to the altar without a mule team!'

'You might consider me,' he offered gently.

'What in the world for?' she said angrily. 'You're the *cause* of all my troubles, not the solution. Let's go and get this other problem over with!'

*   *   *

Beth Hendley had an alarm-clock mind. No matter how late she went to bed, her internal clamour began at exactly six-thirty, rain or shine. She managed to open one eye. A pair of bright blues was staring back at her. Ugly bright blues, with an ugly face behind them.

'What are *you* doing here?' Sue-Ann demanded.

'Me?' Beth fumbled through a list of clichés and found nothing suitable. 'Sleeping, I guess.'

'Sleeping! This happens to be Frank's bed, and he—where is he?'

'Down the hall, love. After the water pipe burst at home, he had the goodness to carry me over and tuck me in with you. He bedded down in the spare room. How about that?'

'Water pipe? What water pipe?'

'Er—in the kitchen. I hope the plumber's been by now.'

'I don't believe a word of it.' Her sister was sitting up in the bed, radiating enough poison to murder half the population of Picayune.

'I find it hard to believe myself,' Beth answered. 'He almost dropped me a couple of times. Then he went back for you. I have no idea how *you* managed to get over here. I think I fell asleep and missed half of what was going on.'

Her sister had the grace to blush. Blonde hair in an artful tangle, blue eyes, a willowy figure, a becoming blush—great day, Beth sighed to herself, what chance does a poor dumpy brunette like me have? But Sue-Ann recognised a life-line when she saw one.

'Oh, something must have warned me,' she said. 'I walked over by myself. Lucky, aren't I, that we're all here.' She gave a shrill little laugh that was close to hysteria. 'If I had been here just by myself wouldn't it have been rack and ruin for my reputation?'

'Right. Rack and ruin,' Beth confirmed cheerfully. A heavy fist banged on the door.

'Breakfast in five minutes,' Frank Wylie bellowed. He opened the door a crack. 'Choice of whatever you want for breakfast. I've got pancakes.'

'Just what I've always wanted,' Sue-Ann said sarcastically. 'What are you going to wear today, Beth?'

'I—I'm not sure,' her sister stammered. The little crack in their fictional excuse was about ten miles wide. No clothing. She could hardly even go down to breakfast in her semi-transparent nightgown.

'Beth, I brought you a robe,' Francis called, still in the hall. 'On the floor beside your bed. It might be a *trifle* large!'

All of which explained why she sat at the breakfast table with her sleeves rolled up further than that, and the skirts of his robe dragging on the floor behind her. The whole thing dipped dangerously low at the bodice despite the fact that she had wound the heavy belt twice around her. But the pancakes were delicious. Even her sister admitted that.

'So I'll stay and do the dishes,' Sue-Ann said, 'while you go on to work.'

'Yes, I'll do that,' Beth responded, rising precariously to her feet.

'And me too,' Frank said, as he grabbed at Beth's swaying figure. 'In fact, I'd better get you back to your house for some clothing.'

'I—yes. What a lovely idea.'

'Oh, but you don't have to go to work,' Sue-Ann wailed. 'You went yesterday.'

'I go every day,' he assured her. 'Working people do that.'

'But—you're an official,' Sue-Ann protested. 'Nobody will give you trouble if you decide to take a day off.'

'You don't understand,' Frank explained. 'I'm the official that *gives* trouble, not *gets* trouble. The school couldn't possibly run if I weren't there to dish it out! Now you just behave yourself, little girl, while your sister and I get on with our labour.'

Sue-Ann received a kiss on her forehead that left her somewhat bemused. 'And you I'll carry,' he murmured in Beth's ear. For some reason she felt cheated. He could just as easily have kissed them both. It couldn't have been a *lot* of trouble.

'You're a lot lighter than you were last night,' he teased as he did a quick turn around the end of the fence. None of the neighbours were in sight for the performance.

'That was the weight of your guilty conscience last night,' she told him firmly. 'You'll require a great deal of praying over this week.'

'All right,' he said, sighing. 'So pray. But isn't that a little sanctimonious?'

It was too hard to keep a straight face. As he set her down on the porch to reach for the door-knob she grinned at him. 'It may be,' Beth Hendley said, 'but I make it a cardinal rule never to use a word I can't spell!'

Despite their efforts, they both arrived at school just in time for the very last bell. Beth, hobbling with a bandage still on her ankle, used her mother's cane to move around with. Nobody in the school seemed to want to make a statement about why a junior history teacher arrived in the Mercedes of the assistant principal. At least not to their faces, they didn't.

Her classes all greeted her with a sigh of relief. 'We had Mr Wylie,' Hoagy Chambers reported. 'Was he born a grouch? What a monster that man is.'

'Never say that,' Beth reprimanded him, but in the back of her mind made a note to jump Hoagy's history grade another two points. A boy that smart deserved some reward. And it was to Hoagy that she turned at the close of school.

'There's a football meeting after school, isn't there?'

'Just a short one,' the young man told her. Hoagy was one of those boys who had outgrown his generation. At sixteen he stood six feet tall, and weighed in at just over two hundred pounds. An amiable black giant, and not too slow, either. 'Skull session. Want something?'

'I want to talk to Billy Joe,' she told him. 'Just for a minute, but it's important. Would you...?'

'You bet I will,' he responded. 'Why don't you wait on the corner of Laurel and Fifth Avenue? I'll make sure he comes by, one way or another, Ms Beth, and then I can go on to my job.'

'Well,' Beth drawled, 'that's part of the problem, Hoagy. I only want to ask him a couple of questions, but I'm afraid he—— '

The big young man stopped her in mid-stride. 'You mean that—that punk might lay a hand on you, Ms Beth?'

'I don't know,' she answered, flustered. 'He might get excited, or something, and——'

'An' I'll stand right behind you. If'n he raises a hand to you I'll cut him off at the pockets.'

'Laurel and Fifth Avenue,' she repeated, smiling for the first time. 'I'll be there.'

The involvement committee held its third meeting of the semester in one of the empty classrooms. Four teachers, two administrators, the principal, and Frank Wylie. It was Dr Wylie this time, in full charge of the operation. He listened to the reports impassively, and when they were all finished he stood up and restlessly paced.

'We've made a good start,' he mused. 'Sixty per cent of the students are enrolled in extra-curricular activities. I wish we had more converts to the drama club. I've got half a dozen senior citizens just looking for a place to volunteer. Carpenters, electricians, sound personnel. There's no end to the resources we can pluck out of the elderly. Now—let's get at the other forty per cent, and make sure we don't lose any of the ones who are already committed. Thank you all.'

'Good meeting,' Ms Margaret, the principal, said as the committee members filed out of the room.

'Partially good,' he mused. 'We said originally that we must not only involve the students, but the teachers and the school committee as well. So how come, when I read down this list of extra-curricular advisers, I find Miss Hendley's name down for seven different jobs?'

'It's because Ms Beth is the one who always steps in where nobody else wants to serve,' the principal commented.

'But she's not married,' one of the other teachers rebutted. 'She has no other ties. Most of the rest of us have families to worry about.'

'Be a shame, wouldn't it,' Frank commented softly, 'if Ms Beth would up and fall in love?'

'Not a chance,' the domestic science teacher remarked. 'Not a chance.'

Frank watched them all file out, a thought plaguing his mind. It was probably just coincidence that he glanced out of the window, and saw the little meeting taking place on the corner of Fifth Avenue, just outside the stadium. But there was a great deal of muttering from the teachers he elbowed aside as he took the stairs two at a time.

*   *   *

The one thing that bothered Beth more than anything else was standing still. She could limp along with practically no problem, using the cane for balance. But standing in one place was more than she could handle. Especially when more than one female student wandered by and made snide remarks.

'Waiting for Dr Wylie, Ms Beth?' After the sixth challenge she was prepared to spit. How did they all know that if she had the choice she *would* be waiting for Dr Wylie? A high school, of course, was as full of rumour and innuendo as a nursing home. In a single day a penny's worth of truth could be amalgamated into a fortune in gossip. So when the two young men came out through the gate she was glad, ever so glad.

There was no hiding Hoagy. He was who he was. But Billy Joe, himself a tall, thin boy, was no pint of peanuts either. And Billy Joe apparently was coming under duress. 'Here he is, Ms Beth,' Hoagy announced.

'I don't wanna talk to you,' Billy Joe growled. 'I got to get home.'

'You *got to* answer me one question,' Beth declared. She folded her hands over her chest and mustered up a glare. Hoagy's hand on Billy Joe's shoulder kept him from walking off.

'You just go ahead and ask,' Chambers urged. 'Billy Joe here, he'll be glad to stand and listen.'

'Damfy will!' Billy Joe exploded. A shake from that massive hand on his shoulder changed his mind. 'So OK. What?'

'A couple of nights ago, Billy Joe, somebody tried to run me down over on Goodyear Boulevard. He was driving a red Cajun Cadillac. Why did you do it?'

'Me?' the boy blustered. 'I don't own no Cadillac. I ain't never driven on Goodyear Boulevard. Never!'

'Never, Billy? There were witnesses, you know.'

'Them kids ain't never gonna say anythin',' the lad retorted. His thin, pimpled chin bobbed, throwing his long red hair askew over his forehead. His face was flushed, perspiring.

'*Them kids* don't have to,' Beth said firmly. 'There just aren't many kids in Picayune with long red hair, Billy Joe. Give it up. Confession is good for the soul.'

'I don't need nothin' done for my soul,' he responded. 'I go to church regular. You can't prove nothin'.'

'Suppose I told the police the licence number of the car?' Beth reached into her purse and pulled out a slip of paper.

'Damn you!' the boy yelled. He snatched at the paper, struggled with her and her purse, then saw something over her shoulder. Before either she or Hoagy could react, Billy Joe had grabbed the paper and was racing up Fifth Avenue, heading for Main Street.

'Shall I chase him?' Frank Wylie was puffing as he came up to Beth. Hoagy was torn between chasing and listening. He chose to listen.

'No,' Beth said. 'There's really no reason why you should. We know who he is.'

'Only he got your paper with the licence plate number on it,' Hoagy commented. 'I'm sorry, Ms Beth. I guess I wasn't much of a guard after all. Did he really...?'

Beth chuckled and patted him on the back. 'You did well, Hoagy. And you too, Mr Wylie. I don't believe I've ever been rescued by two more important people—not since I was out at the Rocket Center and...'

'And what?' Frank coaxed.

'And I got chased by an alligator,' she admitted.

'But you said you had the licence plate of the car that almost hit you,' Hoagy repeated.

'She said that?' Frank Wylie picked her up suddenly by both elbows, and whirled her around behind his back. 'You go ahead, Hoagy. I know you've got an after-school job. And as for you,' he muttered as he turned around to her, 'do you mean to stand there and tell me you had the kid's licence plate number? None of these kids is an infant, you bloody damn fool. He could have done you a lot of harm. Why is it that you have this Messianic impulse? You think you're Supergirl or something?' And by this time he had both hands on her shoulders and her head was wobbling back and forth. 'Or do you have a suicide impulse?' Two more shakes.

Disgusted, Beth summoned up all her remaining strength and swung a punch right at him. It slipped under his guard, landed right on the peak of his nose, and instantly drew blood. 'Dear lord,' he muttered, grabbing for a handkerchief. 'Now look at what you've done!'

'You deserved it,' she announced grandly. 'And the next time you lay your hands on me you'll get worse, *Mr Wylie*.' But her temper was quickly gone. She stepped back a pace, offered him her own little bit of lace, and cocked her head, examining the damage.

'It's not really too bad,' she said, sighing. 'I do have a terrible temper.'

'Almost as bad as mine,' he admitted, dabbing at the end of his nose.

'Why don't we go down to my house and put some ice on it?' she offered. He gestured over to the car park, where his long black Mercedes was still parked.

'Only I just don't understand,' he said as he handed her into the car. 'How can you be so calm when the kid has stolen the licence plate number?'

Beth leaned back against the custom leather, and patted the soft stuffing of the seat-arm. 'What a way to go,' she murmured in admiration. 'Oh—Billy Joe? I didn't tell him I *had* the licence number. I only asked him to suppose what would happen if I had it to give to the police!'

'Cunning,' he acknowledged as he started the engine and backed out into the street. 'And no harm done.'

She settled back in the seat and gave him a solemn look. 'That's what you think,' she said. 'He got away with all my next week's shopping-list!'

CHAPTER SEVEN

AND on the sixth day Beth rested. For part of Saturday, that was. All over Mississippi thousands of teachers caught their breath, slept late, and vowed to find a better-paying job or get married, whichever came first. But Saturday, for Beth Hendley, was an interlude rather than a day off. Along about ten o'clock she went over to the school to do her tutoring, devoted two hours in the afternoon to a new routine for the cheerleaders, and then went shopping out at the North Gate Mall. The pay-cheque she had received on Friday was seriously damaged by Saturday afternoon. Which was mostly responsible for her glum expression when she caught up with her sister—in the kitchen, of course.

A beautifully groomed sister, wearing a pout big enough to launch a Mississippi paddlewheeler. 'About the other night,' Sue-Ann started out.

'Yes, what about the other night?' Beth was too tired to be diplomatic. 'I rate the other night way up there on the catastrophe list, just below the maiden voyage of the *Titanic*.'

'I don't know how I ended up in his bed,' Sue-Ann blustered.

'The devil you don't. You walked there, lady.'

'And so did you,' her sister charged. Beth noted the battle light in her sister's eye, and felt a good fight coming on. It might bring some relief, she told herself, but carried too far could bring catastrophe. Sukey had been off her Valium pills for almost a year now.

'Not exactly, love,' she said, sighing. 'I was carried!'

'He was trying to seduce me!'

'Then how come he ran all the way over here and begged me to rescue him?'

'So it *was* all your idea. I might have known. Busybody! Snoop!' Sue-Ann paced up and down the length of the room, her skirts swirling. Silk, Beth noted. Green silk, with a tight bodice and the skirt cut on the bias, folding around her long, slim legs as she paced. And look at me—an old grey sweatshirt emblazoned 'Property of Ole Miss Athletic Department'. A pair of navy blue sweat-trousers. Nondescript would be the highest label *they* could earn. And a pair of muddy plimsolls that had seen a good many better days. Wearily she sank into a kitchen chair. Lecture-time.

'You know, Sue-Ann, you should never have gone there. Think of what it would have done to your reputation if the neighbours found out. You enjoy the garden club, and the On Stage group, and all the other associations you belong to. How long do you think they would let you continue as a member, with a besmirched reputation?'

'What a drag you are,' Sue-Ann snapped. 'What the devil do you think I was trying to do, attend a bible study class? I was doing my *best* to get him to besmirch my reputation, whatever that means. And I might have succeeded if you hadn't ridden in from out of the west, little Miss Do-Good. If he and I woke up in the same house—not even in the same bed, mind you, but in the same house—there'd be wedding bells for the two of us. And you spoiled it all!'

'You can't be for real,' Beth said, sighing. 'You just can't be. He's not a possum. You can't just declare open season and go hunting him, Sue-Ann. Maybe you two wouldn't suit.'

'We'd suit,' her sister returned grimly. 'Did you know he has six million dollars invested? What woman could *not* suit that sort of income?'

'Six—you've got to be kidding. How——?'

'I asked around,' Sue-Ann returned. 'While you were busy measuring his brain potential, I was busy measuring his pocketbook. Our Mr Wylie made a mint in the National Football League, and unlike a lot of other players he kept it. I understand he has an office up in Jackson where they just try to keep track of all the various businesses he's in!' The girl came to a halt and stared down at her sister. 'And you didn't have the slightest idea, did you?'

'Not the slightest,' Beth admitted dolefully. 'Not that it's important. He doesn't really like me.'

'Oh, he likes you all right. Likes you right in his bed, little sister. And that's something you *won't* do, you hear me?'

'You don't have to shout. I hear you. So?'

'So I'm going to New Orleans for the weekend,' Sue-Ann said impatiently. 'My aunt Eloise has invited me down. I might stay longer. But while I'm gone, you be darn sure that you play least in sight with *my* man. Got it?'

Beth crossed her leg, putting her weak ankle in reach of an exploring hand. It was still sore, but usable. Sue-Ann's man? Probably. And what do I do about it? Nothing, her conscience dictated. Sue-Ann is your sister. If they want each other, then good luck to them both. After all, lots of women are spinsters to the day they die. How else would families have maiden aunts to help with the kids? Dear lord. I don't want to be forever helping other people's kids. I want some of my own! How would that look on my tombstone—'Returned to Sender. Unopened'?

She might have made some comment, but by the time she recovered her senses Sue-Ann had gone, and Fang was barking at the back door for admission. Some day, Beth told herself, Sue-Ann is really going to blow up. That temper can't be contained forever. Like her father. And I'd hate to be the target of the explosion! Wearily Beth got up to open the door.

Fang skidded into the kitchen before the portal was fully open, but Beth hardly noticed. Frank Wylie was standing on the back steps, a big smile on his face. They were a match. He was dressed in grey hand-me-downs, a running-suit that looked as if it might have passed the one-hundred-thousand mark. Perspiration marks stained the armpits, and the back was soaked. 'She's gone?' he asked.

'She? Gone?'

'Great,' he said as he sidled past her. 'Two words in the sentence, and you don't understand either of them?'

'Nobody likes a smart aleck,' Beth grumbled at him, her fatigue evident in the words and in her eyes. 'If you mean my sister, yes, she's gone. Don't tell me you've been doing a Peeping Tom act, waiting for her to leave?'

'Surely I get a cup of coffee before the Inquisition?'

'Surely you'll get a hit——' And all of her mother's long instruction overcame the threat. A lady is a lady is a lady! 'Yes. Of course. Coffee. Black?'

'As usual. My, you look like a worn-out rag.'

'Thank you. You're rather attractive yourself. Sit.'

The coffee-pot had been on for half the day. I should throw it out and make fresh? she debated. But the devil was in her. Let him drink it as it is. Why should I be nice to him? Every time he comes around he's trouble. She banged the coffee-mug down in front of him as if defying him to say something. Anything.

'You spilled coffee on your newspaper.'

'It's *my* paper. And besides, it's yesterday's edition.' But it was also the edition she wanted to read. Warily she moved his mug, picked up the wet copy of the *Item*, and set it aside. 'Now. You came for some reason?'

'I believe so.'

'Well, don't let me detain you. I'm sure you have a dozen other places to be. No?'

'Oh, sit down, Beth,' he said calmly. 'Let me drink my coffee, and then I'm going to take you sailing.'

She sat nervously on the edge of her chair. Why does he have such a strange effect on me? she asked herself. Why do I have this jittery feeling, as if something world-shaking might be about to happen?

'You must be out of your ever-loving mind,' she told him. 'Sailing? It's the first week in October already, you don't own a boat——' Pause for consideration. What had Sukey said? Six million dollars? 'You don't, do you?' she asked cautiously.

He grinned at her, a big, toothy grin that disappeared as fast as it came because he took his first sip of coffee. 'Good grief!' he roared. 'What kind of swill is this?'

'Some of my best coffee,' she offered, lowering her lashes demurely. 'Yesterday's.' And the inevitable guilt load descended on her. 'I could make some fresh?'

'Don't bother,' he sighed. 'My tongue may require a transfusion. I'll check in at the hospital when we come back. No, I don't own a boat.'

'But——'

'But I have a friend.'

'Good for you,' she muttered, *sotto voce*.

He ignored her snide comment. 'But I have a friend who owns a boat, and a house by the water, and he's off to New York for the month, and offered me the use of all of them. Got it?'

'I've—got it. A trusting friend. On the Hobolochitto River?'

'On Hideaway Lake,' he announced, and that grin was back again.

'Great day,' she muttered, and then sat back to regroup. Hideaway Lake. The *ne plus ultra* of Picayune society living. Restricted area, guard posts, houses that cost—even more than that, its own private lodge and club, and a beautiful, quiet lake. 'I used to go skinny-dipping in the Hobolochitto,' she mused. 'A long time ago, of course. It's all—well, not so nice, except where it flows through the Hermitage grounds. But it's too cold.'

'Don't let the Chamber of Commerce hear you say that,' he said, laughing. 'Picayune, the land the sun loves!'

'Ugh.' She shuddered, and rethought her position. 'All right. I'll come, but——'

'So how long will it take you to get ready?'

Probably a hundred years, she told herself frantically, and fell back on her last defence. 'I don't have a thing to wear,' she confessed.

'You look fine to me,' he told her. 'We both look fine. We're going sailing, not slumming. C'mon.'

'But I can't leave Fang alone,' she protested.

'So bring him along. I thought his name was Pansy?'

They were still arguing as he dragged her out of the front door and down the drive, to where his Mercedes waited. Fang, almost wiggling himself to death in his excitement, vaulted into the front seat. Beth found herself, willy-nilly, ensconced in front. Where's your will-power, girl? she yelled at herself. Hit him, or get out, or—dear lord, what am I doing?

He knew, almost as if he could read her mind. 'It isn't will-power you need, lady, it's *won't*-power. And you're not well equipped in that department. Buckle up.'

The car purred over to Goodyear Boulevard, then east to Main Street. Highway Eleven, it was known as outside the few central blocks of the little city. A group of men were gathered around the ancient Shay steam locomotive, parked on a spur of the railroad.

Say something, she commanded herself frantically. 'The Chamber of Commerce is trying to get up a fund to restore the locomotive,' she babbled. 'It was parked there as a memorial, but it's falling apart.'

'Memorial to what?' Like her, he was only making conversation. And the corner of his mouth was twitching.

'Once,' she babbled on, 'this whole section of Mississippi was a logging area. Southern pine, mostly. And the railroad was built to haul the logs down to the sawmills. It's all gone now, and only the engine's left.'

'I read the book.' He laughed. 'It's not all gone. It was the Crosby forests and the Crosby railroad, and the Crosby sawmills. And now you have the Crosby Memorial Library and the Crosby Memorial Hospital— and what else?'

'And the Hermitage,' she sighed. 'That big property that lies in back of all our houses. And the Arboretum. There aren't a lot of Crosbys left. But they did the town proud, didn't they?'

'They did. You do.' He was tooling the big car north, and occasionally staring at her. 'Did anyone ever tell you that?'

'That what?' Dangerous ground, she told herself as she folded her hands neatly in her lap and stiffened her spine.

'That you're a pride to your city, Beth Hendley. You're a joiner and a shaker and a mover. One of the finest and most committed teachers in the city—and altogether the nicest woman I've met in a passel of years.'

'I—haven't done *that* much,' she said, gasping for breath. 'You must have——'

'Not all gossip,' he said, chuckling. 'I suspect I only know ten per cent of the truth. No, you haven't done *everything*, but you're young, Beth. You've years and years to do things in. With me, preferably.'

'With—what?' One of his big hands dropped on top of hers, and patted them gently.

'With me,' he repeated. 'You know—like boy and girl, and all that?'

'You'd better pay attention to your driving,' she said, stiffening. Boy and girl, and all that? He's going to marry Sukey, and—how long does he think I could exist in a town like Picayune, as his mistress? Twenty thousand people live in Greater Picayune. Nineteen thousand of them would know about it by tomorrow week! Here's the time when you change the subject, lady. Quickly!

'I'll bet you don't even know how Picayune got its name, do you?'

'Wow,' he said, chuckling. 'You almost threw me off the track when you went around that curve. No, I don't even know how Picayune got its name, and I'm afraid you're going to tell me.'

'You'd better believe it,' Beth muttered under her breath. And so she did. 'There was a lovely woman who came from around these parts in the 1800s. She was a poet, a writer, and became owner and publisher of the *New Orleans Daily Picayune*. The paper was named after a Spanish coin, worth about six cents—and happened to be the cost of the newspaper.'

'And so when they incorporated the city they named it after the newspaper,' he concluded, with a flourish. 'As it happens, I have a silver picayune in my coin collection.'

'Know-it-all,' she muttered as she sank back into the corner of the car and firmly glued her eyes on what scenery there was.

By the time they reached the furthest north boundary of the city, and wound their way past the guard gate and into the widely scattered housing area, she was feeling miserable. He was Sukey's man, but she hated the thought! He tried once or twice to restart the conversation, but Beth would have no part of it, and Fang spoke only in whimpers. When they arrived at their destination, just after six o'clock, Beth had to acknowledge defeat.

'What a marvellous house,' she said in awe.

'Cottage,' he corrected. 'A summer cottage. Ten rooms, two baths and a shower, central heating——'

'And that's how the other half lives,' she said, sighing. 'Well, perhaps not really a half. The other tenth?'

'It could be easy to get used to,' he judged as he stood beside her, hands in his pockets, and scanned the long reach of the lake. 'Sail first or eat first?'

'Who's cooking?'

'Who else?' he teased. 'Women's work, and all that.'

'Then we sail.' It was impossible to keep a solemn face. She was giggling as he locked on to her elbow and guided her down the grass verge to the dock. Fang, acting as if he had just landed on an undiscovered new planet, raced ahead of them.

The boat was not what she had expected. It was an eighteen-foot-long catamaran, sloop-rigged. The deck was tightly stretched canvas laid over the space between the two hulls. 'You sail, of course?' He bounded on to the deck and reached back a hand to sustain her.

'Doesn't everybody?' she asked airily. The breeze plucked out her most important hair pin, and her curls went sprawling out from her head. Fang, still on the dock, whimpered a refusal. He just could not care for a world which kept rocking under his feet.

'So I'll put him on a long leash,' Frank Wylie decided. Beth, whose whole world seemed composed of rainbows and thunderstorms, barely spared a thought for her poor dog. Instead she struggled forward to the mast and stood there peering out into the troubled sunset. High, racing tatters of clouds. They ought to be telling her some-thing, she thought, but whatever it was would just not come to mind. There was too much else to think about.

'You'll get a good knock if you don't watch for the boom!' he yelled. She turned around and waved at him, just as the sail went up and the stick at its bottom swung in her direction.

Boom, she muttered as she ducked around to the other side of the mast. Beware of the boom. Beware of the pirate too, while you're at it! The boat tilted as the wind caught in the sail. He balanced himself on wide-spread legs, the tiller held lightly in one hand. 'Come on back here!' he yelled.

Beth essayed a walk across the tilted, bouncing canvas, and decided dignity wasn't worth the effort. Crawling was easier.

'Hold her on this course,' he called above the noise of wind and water. 'I'll go forward and run up the jib. Unless you'd care to do that?'

'No—I wouldn't spoil your fun,' she returned as he wrapped both her hands around the oar-like tiller. Run up the jib? And back down again? The man's mad! But he looked so much the berserker Viking that she found

it in her heart to forgive his madness. Besides, he was
so—big and reliable and, yes, handsome. And he doesn't
seem to realise that he's Sue-Ann's man—and so, since
he doesn't think so, and Sukey is in New Orleans, and
we're here all by ourselves on this lovely lake and—oh,
what the hell! And that's something no right-minded
Baptist should say, her conscience dictated. But I'm only
taking a day off, she told herself. It's only one poor little
swear word. And that's the road that leads there, her
conscience retorted. Well-paved, too!

She was able to shrug it all off. He had handled the
jib—which had turned out to be a little triangular sail
just in front of the mast—with great ease, and came
swaying back to her. 'Sit down,' he ordered. She com-
plied. There were times, her mother had told her, when
it did a woman good to let a man think himself superior.
And dominating. Which was a good rationalisation of
the fact that he scared the daylights out of her when he
barked like that.

So she managed to sit on the canvas deck, thankful
that she hadn't worn a dress. And he was down next to
her, shoulder to shoulder, and hip to hip; And isn't *that*
nice, she thought, as she leaned against him. Because
the darn boat was tilted, of course, nothing more.

'I suppose you know all about these waters?' When
she turned her head to ask he was looking down at her,
close enough to kiss.

'Not a bit, Beth. I haven't sailed in years. But you're
well acquainted, I suppose. Pearl River County is full
of waterways.'

She nodded, not willing to trust her voice. Pearl River
was full of waterways, as he'd said, and she had been
on one of them once, so many years ago. A raft trip
that had carried her out into the west branch of the river,
ended up in disaster, and, after considerable cuddling,

had brought her mother to apply a certain form of discipline. And I didn't sit down comfortably for three days, she reminded herself.

'I never realised that sailing could be so—restful,' she commented a few minutes later.

'Is it?' he asked. She looked up at his face again. There were devils in his eyes, and one of his arms had slipped around her, with a hand just inches below her breast.

Oh, lord, she thought, and did her best to move away. Unfortunately the boat was canted even more sharply than before and was bouncing on the scattered, white-flecked waves. His hand would not turn her loose, and she wasn't really sure that she wanted to *be* loose. And so they sailed and sat and enjoyed for another ten minutes before he said something about 'coming about', and proceeded to turn the boat in the other direction.

Another few minutes were required to settle on the new course, and the partially obscured sun was already touching on the trees to the west. The new course evidently required some other changes as well. The boat tilted in the other direction, and now he had to hold her more tightly, more closely, to 'keep you from sliding off', he insisted. It was all so logical. At least, in her dazed condition it *seemed* logical. His arm around her gave a sense of security that filled a gap in her psyche—or was that the right word? He was doing something that nobody had done for years, not since her *own* father died, and it all fitted together. He was so much man that he made her feel much more womanly. So she leaned against him, and paid no attention to the fact that his hand had slipped under her shirt, where it was warmed, as she was.

In fact, not until they were almost back at the dock did it strike her that she wore nothing *under* the sweatshirt, and that his hand was no longer a few inches *below* her breast.

'We've got to come about again,' he called. His errant finger had just climbed her mountain, all the way up to the peak. She squeaked in alarm, bolted away from him and stood up, just as the big stick—the boom—came around and gave her a gentle tap.

'Holy hell!' he yelled as she executed a magnificent swan dive and hit the water. He abandoned the tiller and dived in after her. The little yacht, untended, idled to a halt and gently bumped into the dock. A few feet away Beth came to the surface, shook the hair out of her eyes, and headed off towards the dock in her determined side-stroke. Graceful it was not, but sturdy. Good for ten miles, or a quick kiss, whichever might come first.

There was a rickety wooden ladder at the deep end of the pier—actually, a series of boards nailed over the bollards. Without a bit of trouble she climbed up, stopping just long enough to grab at the bow line of the catamaran. Out in the lake Frank Wylie was diving for the third time, searching, yelling. When he came up for air the next time she decided he had been punished enough.

'Over here!' she yelled, waving an arm. He released a stream of words that turned her ears pink, and then came boiling towards the dock in a crawl that could have set an Olympic record. He hardly used the ladder; it almost appeared that he flew. And then he was squatting down beside her, dripping over everything.

'You liked that,' he grumbled as he wrung out his shirt. 'You enjoyed watching me make a fool of myself.'

It was worth thinking about. She mulled it over in her mind. 'Yes,' she decided. 'I do believe I did.'

'And you can swim like a fish!' A statement, not question.

'Yes, I believe you could say that.'

'So you laughed while I was trying to rescue you?'

'I have to admit that.' Twilight was closing in. She had to lean forward to study his face, and what she saw she didn't like. 'No,' she protested as he stretched and got to his feet.

'I think we both would enjoy another good laugh,' he said ominously. 'The funniest thing I can think of would be that I really *did* have to rescue you. Wouldn't that give you the jollies?'

'No,' she squealed. 'No. No, Frank. No—Francis? I wouldn't——' The rest of the words were lost as he snatched her up and threw her back into the lake.

'It's only a hamburger,' she offered apologetically an hour later. The mosquitoes had come up in swarms as soon as the sun had set. Now the three of them, Frank, Beth and Fang, were settled on the screened porch, looking out over the lake. The veriest trace of a moon was doing its best to make things more cheerful but was having a hard time with the racing high clouds. 'That's all there was in the refrigerator.'

'Good enough.' He reached up for the paper plate, and almost lost his meal as the burger slipped towards the far side. 'No ketchup?'

'No ketchup,' she agreed. 'Want a little mayonnaise?'

'Mayonnaise on a hamburger? Heaven forbid! You look very attractive in that towel, love. Is that the sarong style?'

'Don't mock me,' she snapped. 'A girl can hardly look her best dressed in an old beach towel. At least you found some shorts to wear.'

'Well, can I help it if my friend George didn't entertain many female guests out here?'

'You don't know your friend as well as you think you do,' she muttered. 'He's got plenty of female clothing in his cupboards, but they're all too—too small for me.'

'Hard to believe.' That laugh was chasing around his eyes again. 'You're not all that big.'

'In—certain areas I'm not all that small,' she retorted indignantly, and then turned blush-red as he roared in laughter.

'I surrender, Beth. When you're right, you're right. Did you find anything to drink?'

'Water?'

'Beer.'

Yes, she wanted to say, there's plenty of beer in the fridge, but if you think I'm going to sit out here miles from anywhere, dressed in a towel, and serve you beer, you've got another think coming, man. Several thinks, for that matter. This is one occasion when alcohol and Beth Hendley just don't mix!

'OK, water.' He sounded less than enthusiastic, which fazed her not at all.

'Ice water,' she informed him moments later when she padded back out on to the veranda. He was suitably impressed. From across the water she could hear music; a band was playing at the Lodge.

'Dance?'

'No. I'm tired.' She sank back into one of the lounge chairs and put her feet up. 'It's been a long, hard day. We ought to be getting back.'

'As you say, a long, hard day,' he mused. 'Why don't we stay overnight? Plenty of empty rooms, empty beds?'

'And just what do you mean by that?' She jumped to her feet. All night she had been waiting for just those words. The first step off the road and into seduction. 'What kind of a girl do you think I am, Mr Wylie?'

'I wish I knew,' he grumbled. 'Why don't you yell a little louder? The next house is barely two acres away. They wouldn't want to miss anything.'

'You don't catch me with that line!' She spat out the words, standing like some young Athena, legs akimbo, hands on hips—until her towel slipped and she had to make emergency repairs.

'No, I can see I don't. How old are you, Beth?'

'Old enough to know better,' she snapped. 'I want to go home now.'

'Of course you do.' He pulled himself up to his feet. Fang, who had been dozing in the corner, came awake with a rush and gambolled forward to join the fun. Beth, startled as both the man and the dog seemed to stalk her, backed away a step or two, and then whirled and ran. Frank Wylie stopped to laugh. Fang jumped at the mysterious cloth his mistress was trailing, set his teeth firmly in the bottom hem of the towel, and dug in his heels.

Like an alabaster statue being unveiled at its dedication ceremony, Beth Hendley felt the knot at her breast being worried away, tried vainly to stop running to relieve the pressure, and found that two hands were not enough to snatch at her only covering as it fell at her feet. The three of them, woman, man and dog, came to a complete halt, staring.

'You're still not speaking to me, Beth?'

'Not a word. Turn right here. How in the world am I going to get into the house without being seen?'

'It's dark enough,' he assured her. 'I'll just stop in front of the house and carry you in.'

'I can walk, thank you, Mr Wylie.'

'No, you can't. We lost both of your shoes in that second dive.'

'I didn't dive,' she snarled. 'I was pushed. Lord, what a mean man you are.'

'Isn't it so? Are you sure that towel will hold all right?'

'I certainly don't want to get back into my soaked running-suit.'

'I suppose it's not enough for me to say I'm sorry.'

'It wouldn't be if you meant it,' she snapped. 'But look at you. You're still laughing. No, it won't be enough. Are you sure you won't be able to finish your programme here in Picayune——?'

'And go away?' he interrupted. 'Not a chance. I've signed on for the complete school year. Then I'm off to Baltimore to study the results. It'll make a good book, Beth.'

'Ms Hendley, if you please.' And why does that wrench at my heart? she wondered as she brushed the tear from her eye. Mad tears, not sad. Maybe if I could just get through one day without getting mad at him we might possibly have got along. But—I wonder if all the men from Baltimore act the way he does? If I were in my right mind I'd whack him over the head with a frying-pan. Or a rolling-pin!

'And now what are you thinking?' he asked cheerfully as he pulled his car up in front of her house. 'Some new way to roast me for dinner?'

'If you must know,' she said huffily, 'I'm trying to figure out how to be forgiven for all the things and thoughts and words that *you* caused me to—to... No, don't get out. I'll walk for myself.'

She opened the door of the car and stepped out, only to cut the arch of her foot on one of the sharp pebbles. It was too much. She fell back into the car, crying out her rage.

'So I'll carry you?' he suggested in a very tentative voice. She sniffed back the last two tears and leaned around to look at him. He sounded most unsure of himself, and that was something new indeed.

'I—would you, please?' she managed in a very little-girl sound. 'I—don't seem to have control of my legs. I—hope nobody sees us. This towel is just not much of a—lord, how did I ever get into such a mess?'

'Just hold on, Beth,' he said as he slid out from behind the wheel and walked rapidly around to her side of the car. He was still wearing the tight shorts from his friend's wardrobe, and a pair of rubber clogs, held on in Japanese fashion by a thong between his toes.

'I'm holding,' she half whispered. He was only a black shadow moving against the blacker night. It was easier to deny to a shadow that you loved him. Because, she knew, that's just what all this fumbling and fainting and hurting are all about. I love him. Lord, why should it happen to me? And Sukey wants him!

He bent to slip an arm under her knees, and grunted as he accepted her full weight. 'You seem a lot heavier than you were last time,' he grumbled. 'You must have put on a lot of weight.'

'In three days? What's the trouble?'

'I can't keep this damn clog on my foot,' he mumbled as he shifted her weight slightly. 'Now, that's better.'

'Hurry up,' she muttered. 'Somebody might see us.'

'Not a chance,' he assured her, just as the searchlight came on behind them, pinning them against the car with its brilliant spot. And the voice was the same. Sergeant Matthews.

'Well,' said the officer. 'Making a habit of it, are we? And this time you're only wearing a towel, Ms Beth?'

'I can explain,' she said, slumping wearily against Frank's strong chest.

'I doubt that,' the sergeant responded as he pulled his notebook out and set one foot up on the bumper of

Frank's car, to make himself a writing-table. 'I sure to heaven doubt that, but it ought to be interesting listening to you try.'

'Surely you don't mean to make a federal case of this?' Beth snapped. 'We have a right to—well, to do almost everything. Of what are you accusing us?'

'If that ain't like a schoolteacher,' the old sergeant sighed. 'Of what are you accusing us? I'm not accusing you of anything, Ms Beth. I'm scouring the town, along with the rest of our patrols, to let everyone know that Tropical Storm Ophelia has been upgraded to a hurricane, and right at the moment it's heading directly for Mobile, Alabama with winds of ninety-five miles an hour. Got it?'

'I've got it,' Beth said, shaking her head sadly. The whole world was out to oppress her. Wylie and the sergeant were not enough, so God was sending a hurricane! Her faith wavered just the slightest bit.

'Mr Wylie,' she said morosely, 'do you suppose you might carry me inside?'

CHAPTER EIGHT

'You don't look too good, Ms Hendley,' young Hoagy commented. It was Monday afternoon, and Beth could hardly decide whether to laugh or to cry. Sunday had been the worst day of her life. She had awakened in shame, and hadn't the courage to go to church services. And now Monday hadn't been a great deal better. The high, fleeting dark clouds, precursors of the wandering hurricane, matched her mood.

'*Well*,' she corrected automatically. 'I may not look too well. My being *good* hasn't anything to do with how I look.'

The boy gave her a big grin. Lectures went right over his head, as did English corrections. And *double entendres*. 'If you say so, ma'am. They want to see you in the principal's office.'

Beth sighed as she rubbed her head. There was the beginning of an ache forming just behind the bone. Sukey hadn't come home, and Aunt Eloise had called from New Orleans, asking where she might be. Coming home dressed in a towel wasn't the high point of my career, either, she told herself glumly.

'Someone wants to see me? Who?'

'I don't know,' he said. 'Billy Joe and his ma and his aunt—like that. And the principal too, of course.'

'Of course.' Beth sighed as she crammed her mark-book and everything else she could think of that might be pertinent into her battered briefcase. Thank heaven Frank Wylie isn't included. How many times did he tell me *not* to send that warning report? Damn the man. A totally disreputable, conniving—Yankee! And yet—she sat frozen at her desk. And yet I love him, she meant to say! Beth shrugged her shoulders and shook her head. Books were full of it, weren't they? Girls who fell in love with the wrong man? Dear lord!

Talking to herself, she went out into the empty corridor. 'There's another good joke on life,' she muttered to herself. When they had a fire drill it took fifteen minutes to empty the building. But when the principal had come on the public address system and announced that the school was closing early due to the hurricane, the whole six hundred or so students just seemed to—disappear. Vanish!

The school secretary was pounding away on the keyboard of her word processor. She lifted her head for just a minute and grinned. 'They're all inside.' She gestured with her head towards the closed door.

Billy Joe was sitting on the plain bench just beside the door. The 'sinner's seat', it was known as throughout the school. The place where students awaiting disciplinary action were left with time to think about their sins. He looked up at her, his long, narrow face painted into a glare, his straggly red hair hanging down in all directions. Maybe someone ought to tell the kid, Beth thought, that he could run faster if he had his hair cut. But she had her own troubles. She reached for the doorknob.

Ms Margaret Lewis came around her desk with a welcoming smile on her face. Two elderly women were sitting side by side at the small conference table tucked into the corner of the office.

'And this is our Ms Hendley,' the principal announced proudly. 'Beth, these are Mrs Crutch and Mrs Mowbray. They've come in to school to consult about Billy Joe.'

Mrs Mowbray looked like her son. A narrow face, forty-five going on sixty, with curls that gave her a doll-like appearance. Red curls, somewhat darker than her son's, perhaps with a little chemical encouragement?

'She's the one out to get my Billy Joe,' Mrs Mowbray said truculently. Mrs Crutch nodded agreement.

'That's a serious charge,' the principal said. 'Ms Beth is one of our best teachers. In fact she's won several awards in the past four years. Why don't we all sit down? Our *Dr* Wylie will be along any minute now. I always think it best to have a man involved in situations such as this, don't you?'

Both the other women nodded agreement. Mrs Crutch licked her lips. Looking for some place to bite, Beth thought. And you, Ms Margaret—you always thought it best to have a *man* about? When did *that* belief start? Tomorrow? Margaret Lewis had long been noted as a disciplinarian who never ever required a *mere male* to back her up. If any motto suited her, it would have been 'walk sternly and carry a big stick'! But the game promised to be interesting. This principal was noted for backing her teachers, if they were right, to the hilt and beyond. Beth settled back in one of the chairs, prepared to out-wait the opposition. The two ladies glared at her from across the table, as if she were already convicted and ready for execution.

Frank Wylie came into the room with a rush. 'Sorry to be late,' he offered. 'And, Ms Margaret, the chairman of the school board is outside wanting to see you.'

'Then I'd better go. You'll excuse me, ladies? Dr Wylie will handle the discussion.' And with that she whisked out the door.

'You must be Mrs. Mowbray,' Wylie said. 'I recognised you because of your hair. It's much like Billy's. Do make yourself comfortable.'

Beth shook her head. *Dr* Wylie, doubly emphasised. Flattery will get you everywhere. My Bachelor of Science degree isn't worth a nickel in armed conflict! The seating resolved itself. Frank Wylie took the chair at the head of the table. If the man had a toga he would look like Pontius Pilate, Beth thought and grimaced. The two outsiders grouped themselves on the far side of the table, leaving Beth alone to face them all.

Frank Wylie must have caught her thought. He gave her a big grin, partially concealed from the visitors. 'Now, I haven't had a chance to review this file in detail,' Wylie said as he thumbed his way through a thick folder. 'Mrs Mowbray? How is it that your son transferred to Picayune from Hattiesburg?'

It wasn't the question the mother had anticipated. 'Why——' she stuttered. 'Why, there was a cabal of teachers down there who didn't like my Billy Joe. He has a wonderful brain——'

'And barely escaped his freshman year with a minimum passing average,' Frank interrupted. 'Sixty-five per cent, to be exact. The lowest possible passing grade in any school system in Mississippi.' For just a second Beth was proud of him. Since Saturday night, when he had brought her home dressed modestly in a large bath towel, that hadn't been the case. To be frank, she had spent a long and restless weekend because of *Mr* Frank Wylie. And just as soon as she could muster the courage she meant to have a serious discussion with the hateful man! And there was nothing to say you couldn't hate a man that you loved. Where was that written?

'Well, as I said, the teachers were all against him,' Mrs Mowbray said truculently. 'So I sent him up here to his Aunt Amelie. And look what happens. Immediately he falls into the hands of this—this person.'

'Imagine that,' the big man at the head of the table commented. He fumbled through more papers, his lips pursing in and out as he concentrated. 'Ah—here. Miss Hendley, what is Billy Joe's average in your history class? No—wait just a minute. Perhaps we'd better have the young man in to join the discussion.' He reached over behind him, where a buzzer was connected on the principal's desk, and pushed the button.

A moment later Billy Joe was ushered in. He came angrily, but stopped abruptly when he saw Frank Wylie sitting in the centre chair. 'Sit by your mother,' Wylie instructed. For a second it seemed the boy might refuse, but then he saw the glint in the big man's eyes, and went obediently around the table. His mother tried to hold his hand; he shook it off.

'Now, then, Miss Hendley?'

'We are in our fourth week,' Beth recounted softly. 'Five weeks to go until the quarterly examinations. To date Billy Joe's average is fifty-two per cent.' Silence weighed heavily on the group.

'That ain't my fault,' the boy protested. 'What do I wanna know about George Washington for? All I wanna do is run!' He shook his head, as if unable to understand the adult view. 'It's your fault. You're a lousy teacher. I don't need no history to play football!'

'The boy comes home regular every night and studies for hours,' Mrs Crutch intervened. 'Never saw a boy study the way he does.'

And here, Beth told herself angrily, it's time to pull the plug. 'Mrs Crutch,' she said, 'in my class I give homework assignments three times a week. To date Billy Joe has never completed a single assignment.'

The assembled relatives stared at her as if she were some assistant devil. 'I didn't know we was supposed to hand in no papers,' the boy muttered.

Beth dug into her briefcase, pawed around for a moment, and then handed a paper to Frank Wylie. 'During the second week of school this year, Billy Joe,' she explained, 'you were doing so poorly that I went out of my way to explain to you about homework papers.'

'I didn't know.'

'And to make sure you knew,' Beth continued relentlessly, 'I had you write and sign a statement at the bottom of the paper that you *did* understand!' The boy ducked his head, unwilling to meet any of the eyes around the table.

Another silence. 'And I see here,' Frank continued, 'that you have a forty-three average in English, a thirty-seven average in math, and—all your marks are the same, aren't they, Billy Joe?'

'I don't care,' the boy muttered. 'Ain't nothin' important in any of them things. All I wanna do is run. Just you let me run the football, and keep out of my way! I'm gonna be rich and famous, and play in the National Football League. You been there, Mr Wylie. Ain't that the way it is?'

Beth recognised it for what it was: an appeal to Caesar. All the boy could see was that narrow little corridor that led to success in football, and Frank Wylie had been there. She held her breath, waiting for his answer.

'No, that's not all it is.' The big man sighed. 'Sometimes I wish it were. There's a lot more to it than just running, Billy Joe. A lot more. And your first hurdle is that you have to graduate from high school.'

'With a sixty-five per cent average,' Beth added.

'Yes, with a sixty-five per cent average,' Frank confirmed. 'But first, you have to pass your present courses. *You* have to do it!'

'I don't understand,' Mrs Crutch said. 'He's home every night, and he works hard at his school stuff, and——'

'I don't know about the other school nights,' Beth interrupted. 'But I'm sure he's not home on Wednesday night. Every week I go to church on Wednesday night, and Billy Joe is out there on Goodyear Boulevard when I go in, and when I come out.'

'That's not possible,' Mrs Mowbray snapped. 'I talk to my boy every night by telephone at eight o'clock. Every night! You couldn't have seen him. Not possible!'

'Isn't that strange?' Frank countered. 'I saw him myself just last Wednesday, him and that bright red Cajun Cadillac of his. It made me pretty angry. I was almost ready to call the police.'

'Don't be silly,' the boy's aunt spat. 'Billy Joe's only sixteen. He don't have no car, and no licence either, for that matter!'

'Do you say so?' The big man pushed himself back into his chair, and unbuttoned his blazer.

'If he doesn't have a car,' Beth broke in, 'there must be somebody else in that crowd that looks just like Billy.'

'But that wouldn't be hard to find out,' Frank Wylie said softly. 'I have the licence plate of the car we're talking about. What I think I'll do is turn it over to the police department. Probably the car is stolen... And probably it was the car that tried to run Miss Hendley down last Wednesday night,' Frank Wylie added after a moment's pause. 'And put her in the hospital. I think I'd *better* call the police!'

'But——' Mrs Mowbray stuttered.

'But somebody during this meeting,' Frank said as he stood up and tapped the table, 'has been lying. Several somebodies. There's nothing I hate worse than liars. Did you have something else to say, Mrs Mowbray?'

The woman glared at him but shook her head.

'Mrs Crutch?'

No answer.

'Then I suggest to you both that you light a fire under this young man before he flunks out of school, ladies. Because if he does that, he'll never run a football again, not anywhere in his life. Believe me, I know. After nine years in the National Football League myself, I'm well aware that there's no place for stupidity there!'

'Wait.' Beth could not let it all end on such a note. 'How about baseball, Billy Joe? To make it in football you not only have to graduate from high school, but you have to graduate from college as well. In baseball there's the possibility you could be selected right out of high school!'

'Ain't got no interest in baseball,' the boy returned as he stood up, snarling. 'Just football. And if you squeal to the police about me or—about me, you'll be sorry!'

'Then let me have the last few words,' Frank Wylie offered. 'As of this moment, Billy Joe, you are suspended from all athletic participation in this school, and will remain suspended until all your grades are brought up to at least sixty-five per cent.'

'I'll take this up with the school board,' Mrs Crutch said as she pushed back her chair and made for the door. Mrs Mowbray followed. Billy Joe hesitated, then started to follow. His tough image was failing him. Behind the glare, the mumbled words, there was a tiny tear in his eye. The boy was projecting from behind the young man's face.

'You could join our tutoring group,' Beth offered.

'I don't need no tutorin',' the boy snarled. 'And just you watch, trouble-maker.'

'Billy Joe.' The flat statement of his name whirled the boy around to face Frank Wylie. The man put one huge hand on the boy's shoulder. 'Let's understand each other,' he said softly. 'Ms Beth is *my* woman. Anybody gives her trouble, I'm gonna grind his bones into little splinters. Very little splinters. Got it?'

Another set of defiance held on the boys lips, and then faded away.

'Got it?' Frank repeated.

'I got it,' the boy mumbled, and hurried out of the room.

Beth almost collapsed on the top of the conference table, her head tucked into her arms. There was nothing worse in the world for her than this sort of confrontation. She felt a warm hand on her shoulder.

'It had to be said. You were right weeks ago, and you're right now, Beth.'

'I might be right,' she said bitterly, 'and still be wrong. Lord, how I hate all you sports people.' She shook his hand off and struggled to her feet, crying. 'You heard the boy. All he wants to do is run! That's his whole ambition. And he's good at it, isn't he?'

'Yes, he's good at it. But——'

'But he'll never make it, will he?' she snapped as she dabbed at her tears. 'If he were a baseball player some team might draft him and send him to their farm league, and teach him enough to do well. But football and basketball? Not a chance. The NFL and the NBA are too miserly to fund their own farm teams, so they draft from colleges. And the poor dumb kids who can't make it on their own through college—what happens? They *might* be admitted to some football factory. Some college that hires teams and doesn't really give a damn—oh, I'm sorry—doesn't care at all for the boys, it just cares to keep its stadiums full. And in the doing it teaches the kids that it's all right to lie and cheat and steal and do drugs!'

He offered his handkerchief. She needed it. Her eyes were overflowing like Niagara Falls. 'And poor kids like Billy Joe who can't even master high school, what about them? The only way Billy Joe is going to make that is if all the teachers in this school lie for him. And I can't compromise my principles that much.'

She forced his handkerchief back into his hand. 'So we're just like Gilbert and Sullivan,' she raved at him. 'I'm right and you're right and the leagues, they're all right, but poor Billy Joe goes down the drain!'

'Not all the leagues and colleges are like that,' he murmured. 'Some, but not all.' Those big strong arms came around her, and she found her head nestled against his chest, deep in the warmth and comfort that she really wanted.

'And besides,' she muttered into his shirt front, 'I'm *not* your woman!'

'Damned if that's so,' he returned, squeezing gently. 'You *are* my woman, Beth Hendley, and I don't want to hear any more arguments out of you on that score, or——'

'Or you'll beat up on me?' Barely a whisper, that, but he caught it and chuckled.

'You'd better believe it. Like this.' He squared her around, tipped up her chin, and leaned down. I'm not his woman, she kept telling herself as his lips enclosed her, shut out the world, sparked both contentment and revolution at the same time. I'm not his—and a deep sigh. Yes, I am his woman, if only he really wants me! And for the moment she believed it entirely, and had not a whisker of a thought for her missing sister.

'Oh, is the conference over?' Margaret Lewis walked into her own office with her back turned to the couple by the table, and proceeded over to the windows. 'My, it looks to be a big storm coming. I've always liked storms, myself, but not really big ones. A good wind seems to clear the air, don't you think?' And by that time Beth and Frank had sprung apart, each wearing guilt signs a mile high.

'Yes,' Frank said, but he had to clear his throat a couple of times to make it sound distinct.

Margaret Lewis was nobody's fool. She chuckled as she swung around. 'Yes to what? The conference or the weather?'

'Or both,' Wylie rumbled in that big, deep voice that seemed to match his size. 'We and the Mowbrays agreed to disagree, I suspended Billy Joe from all athletics until his marks are closer to passing, they all threatened to take the matter up with the school committee, Ms Beth gave me a hard time for insensitivity, so I kissed her to prove otherwise. It's a nice habit; I think I'll do it more often. As for the weather, I haven't been in Picayune all that long.'

'Well, I don't know about all that,' Ms Margaret responded. 'I think there's something in the rules about non-fraternisation between teachers and administrators. But you do make a nice pair, and just so long as you don't keep it up in front of the students, I'll not say a word. Now, about the hurricane?'

'I think I'd better go home,' Beth managed to squeeze in, feeling her anger rise again. 'My dog needs feeding, and my sister's missing, and—there's the hurricane and all.'

'Devoted to me, she is,' he commented solemnly as she headed for the door. 'Can't do a thing without me.'

She stopped just long enough glare at him. 'Stop it! You just plain stop it—Francis.' All she earned was a broad grin.

* * *

By six o'clock that night Hurricane Ophelia, a late-season marvel, had moved into first place on the hit parade. All the television and radio stations were broadcasting warnings. The storm centre was still some three hundred miles away, almost stopped in position, but threatening the Gulf Coast between Biloxi and Gulfport, altogether too close to Picayune to make pleasant thinking. And Sukey had yet to be heard from. As for Fang, he was restless under the pressure of the coming storm, and had completely given up answering to the name Pansy.

'All right, Fang,' Beth called as she put down the telephone for the fifth time. Sue-Ann was definitely not in New Orleans. Perhaps she had never been there. And the state police had no record of an accident that might have involved her.

So Beth and her dog wandered out to the front porch for another look. Sunset was highlighting the mare's tails of clouds running before the storm itself. The wind was gusting, tugging at the trees, rattling at the loose garage door, and then banging at the shutters on her windows. They hadn't been closed in a dog's age. Slowly, reluctant to lock herself into a dark house, she went about the job. The gusting wind tore at the boards in her hands but the job had to be done. By morning the storm would be too close to allow her to do anything with her puny strength.

'In fact,' she muttered, 'I can hardly close them now. What I need is——'

'A man to do your muscle-work for you,' he said from just behind her.

She whirled around and reached for him hungrily. 'Oh, Frank—Francis,' she called to him over the noise of the sighing wind. 'I've——'

'Never been so glad to see me before,' he interrupted, gathering her up off her feet, laughing as he did so.

'What a tiny packet of peanuts you really are, Beth Hendley. Why is it that when you're mad you seem to be ten feet tall?'

Her head was buried in the cup of his neck, her hands around his neck, clinging with all her strength. 'Witchcraft,' she said directly into his ear. 'All we girls learn that at our mother's broom—er—knee.'

'I wish I could have known your mother,' he replied as he swung her around in a wide circle that brought forth a squeal of alarm. And a sharp bark from Fang, who was back in his aggression mode again.

'I wish you could have, too,' she told him as he gradually slowed the whirl and brought her feet back down on the ground. 'She would have loved you. Are you going to stand there, or are you going to close the shutters?'

'I thought I'd kiss you first.'

She pushed away from him, laughing. 'Oh, no, you don't. I know you men. Around these parts you do the work first, and *then* get your reward.'

'*Re*ward?' he asked, putting the accent on the first syllable as she had.

'Well, maybe my mother wouldn't like you all that much,' she teased. 'She was a Daughter of the Confederacy! My great-grandfather fought at Stone Mountain.'

'Great,' he said as he swung her up in his arms again. 'My grandparents didn't come over from the old country until 1921, and being a true barbarian, I'm going to kiss you now!'

'And what, may I ask, is going on here?'

Beth, looking over his shoulder, her cheeks red with laughter, almost swallowed her tongue. 'Sukey,' she gasped.

'Why, I should think it's fairly obvious,' Frank answered for her. 'I'm kissing the woman. Or rather, I was about to. If you wouldn't mind waiting just a minute or two, I'll get it done and then we can have a long talk.'

'Don't you dare——'

'Look, Sue-Ann, your sister looks petite, but to be honest its pretty hard holding her up like this. Now you just wait your turn.' With which he whirled around until his back was to the blonde, and went about the kissing business. Beth closed her eyes and hung on. It seemed the only appropriate thing to do. After all, if he was intent on kissing her, Sukey or no, there wasn't much Beth Hendley could do about it, was there? That bit of rationalising managed to hold her for a second or two, after which his lips did the rest.

Did the rest so well, in fact, that not until the second blow shook his body and he stopped kissing and began cursing, did she realise that all was not well. Sukey, with an old broom in her hands, was whaling away at him with all her strength.

'What the hell——?' he roared, but he took the time to set Beth down and push her to one side before he turned to defend himself. 'What in the name of all that's holy do you think you're doing, girl?' One of his massive hands caught the broom in mid-stroke, and then snapped it in half before he threw it over the banister. 'Just what the hell are you up to?' If it hadn't been for the noise of the gathering storm, he was yelling loud enough to be heard all the way out to McNeill.

'I'm going to break your head!' Sukey yelled back. Her face was contorted, ugly. 'And then I'm gonna break hers too. Nobody steals my man, don't you know that, damn you? I told her to leave you alone. Damn you both.' The blonde was almost frothing at the mouth as she frantically searched the porch for some other weapon. 'Nobody, but nobody, takes my man! Nobody!'

'Oh, no,' Beth moaned. 'Sukey.'

'And don't you try to make up to me, Beth Hendley. You're no sister of mine! If Daddy were only here he'd——'

'Now wait just a damn minute,' Frank said. He advanced on the blonde and enveloped her, holding her so tightly she could hardly move a muscle. 'First of all, I've never said a word or done a single thing to make you think I was interested in you. Secondly, Beth is my woman, and I don't intend to stand by and let you abuse her. It seems to me that you've been riding on her back for years, Sue-Ann. And now you're going to have to get off. Beth and I are going to marry. There'll be no place for you and your ugly temper in our home. Got it?'

He held her shoulders while he extended his arms to full distance and set her down. Sue-Ann's face was pale in the gathering darkness. Pale, distorted, twisted. She broke loose from his grip, tears running down her face. Fang chose that moment to enter the fray. One swift kick from her pointed shoes sent the animal yapping into the corner.

'Don't you dare touch my dog!' Beth yelled. Sukey took one look at the avenger approaching, spat at them, and ran for the drive. 'Oh, dear lord, no,' Beth moaned as she clung to one of the roof posts and watched. Sukey was into the car, the motor roared, tyres screamed, and she was gone.

'Well, thank heaven for that,' Frank Wylie said as he came over beside her and dropped a comforting arm around her shoulders.

'Dear lord, no.' Beth shivered and leaned back into the warmth of him.

'It's over, Beth, and no harm done.'

'You don't know.' She was crying gently. 'I—don't mean to get your shirt wet, Francis, but—you don't know.'

'So you'll tell me,' he coaxed. 'It's starting to sprinkle. Tell me.'

'Let me look at Fang,' she muttered, and slipped away from him. Her dog was huddled in the far corner, still whimpering, but he came out to his mistress and cuddled close. 'I think he's all right.'

'Then come back here and tell me,' he insisted. It was truly dark by this time; she could see the huge bulk of him sitting on the swing, idly pushing it back and forth with one foot. She went, carrying Fang in her arms. There was time to adjust, time to set the little dog down, time to nestle into the warm shelter he made for her. His thigh touched hers, offering more excitement than comfort. His arm came around her again. 'Now, about Sue-Ann?'

'She's not——' Beth fumbled for words. 'She has a problem, Francis. A small psychological problem. She's been under treatment for years. I thought she was getting better, but her father—my stepfather...'

'Her father what?'

'Her father committed suicide. Sukey found him—in the garage. She has never forgotten. She's a sensitive girl anyway, and with that——'

'Oh, brother,' he muttered. 'And you've had to put up with this all this time?'

'Of course,' Beth said indignantly. 'She's my sister. My mother asked me to look after her. And now she's gone off—and there's no telling what she'll be up to next. She's liable to do almost anything. I think she's been drinking. I'm scared.'

'No need to be.' He shifted his weight and drew her closer. 'I'm going to spend the night with you.' Just a day earlier such an announcement would have sent Beth up into the tree-tops out of anger. Now it sounded so—nice. She leaned her head back. 'Tell you what,' he went on. 'Maybe I'd better notify the police department, just in case.'

He was gone into the house before she could think of an answer. Gone into the kitchen, in fact, all the way through to the other side of the house. So when the lights of the several cars came racing up Third Avenue and swung into her drive she could not help but scream.

The lights, three sets of them, glared at her, pinning her on to the swing like a butterfly on a display. Doors slammed. She screamed again. The several indistinct figures were out beside the trucks, throwing things in her direction. Their aim was not too good. Two of the missiles splattered at her feet before the third struck her in the stomach and broke. Eggs. Fresh eggs. She screamed again.

Fang finally showed his courage. He vaulted off the swing and went charging down on to the drive, growling as he went. Somebody in the area of the cars laughed. Not for long.

The screen door behind Beth slammed open. 'Are you OK?' Frank Wylie grated. She waved a hand and he was gone, thundering down the stairs like an army tank in battle array. One of the three drivers saw the danger and jumped back into his vehicle. The other two hesitated for just a moment too long. Frank roared a challenge, smashed into both drivers, picked one up and threw him at the side of his truck, and then snatched at the other. The first driver gunned his engine and screamed back out into the street. The second driver lay where he had fallen, beside his vehicle. And the third driver hung there in Frank's hands, being shaken so that his head bounced back and forth without control.

'Frank!' Beth, released from her fears, sprang up and dashed down towards the combatants. 'Frank!' Her attempt to stop him by grasping his steel arm was hopeless. 'Frank!' she yelled at him. 'You'll kill him!'

The rage gradually faded from Wylie's face, but he still held the driver by the scruff of the neck. 'Yeah,' he said. 'I wanted to for just a minute there. Are you all right?'

'I'm—I'm all right,' she murmured. 'They were throwing eggs. I've got a little of it on me—but I'm all right. Who is this?'

'Who else?' he said gruffly. 'Billy Joe. And one of his friends. I don't know who that one is. Not a student at the school, I would guess. Look, love, go call the police. And tell them we'll need an ambulance.'

Beth hurried into the house. It took time to get her fingers untangled. The noises at the other end of the line soothed her. She put the instrument down gently, took her first deep breath in the last twenty minutes, and walked slowly back out to where Frank guarded the two prisoners. Sirens sounded in the distance, and the police were on the scene. Frank explained it all. Beth had all she could do to stand close, her arm tucked in under his elbow, shivering.

And when they were gone he led her back up into the house, with Fang close behind. Almost by habit they went to the kitchen. 'I'm a mess,' she said, sighing.

'You look fine to me,' he responded, and she was back in the comfort of his arms again.

'I'm glad it's over. Why eggs?'

'They'll stain the house,' he explained. 'It won't come off. The whole area will have to be washed down, and then repainted.'

'Oh, lord,' she muttered. 'I can't afford that.'

'That's not the important part,' he told her softly, as one hand smoothed her hair.

'Important part?'

'Those kids were over on Goodyear Boulevard, as usual. Somebody came by and pointed them at us. Offered them each fifty dollars if they'd come by. Somebody.'

'No,' Beth gasped. 'She's my sister. She wouldn't do a thing like that!'

'Wouldn't she?' Before she could answer he put one hand behind her head and buried her against his chest. 'No more, love. You've had enough of a day today. Come on now, let's get you into the bath tub.'

CHAPTER NINE

THE storm played ducks and drakes with Picayune all night. High, thin tatters of clouds raced across the moon and were gone. Occasionally a cluster of thunderclouds, lower than the racing clouds, would wander into sight, smash at the streets with a rain assault, and whistle away on a northwesterly course. Beth, bathed and clothed in a robe and warm flannel nightgown, could not bear to be confined inside with all the shutters closed.

So they moved outside on to the swing again, sitting close together with Fang at her feet, and a portable radio tuned to a New Orleans all-night station in front of his. Frank Wylie was like a beacon in the night, sustaining her with one casual arm around her shoulders, offering conversation when needed.

'But you don't understand,' Beth said for the tenth time.

'Probably not. Tell me about it again.'

'Don't mock me. You just don't understand Sukey.'

'I couldn't argue with that.'

'She's always been—sensitive. Even *I* didn't understand her for the first couple of years. But then—well, she became my sister, don't you see? You *have* to love your sister. Everybody knows that.'

'The latest storm bulletin,' the radio muttered. 'Hurricane Ophelia is now at a standstill about two hundred miles off the coast. If she proceeds on her presently projected course she is expected to come ashore between New Orleans and Gulfport. Maximum storm winds are one hundred and five miles an hour. In a related story, Hinson Oil Platform Number Six has evidently collapsed under the force of the winds. Three men were still on that platform at midnight. Stay tuned.'

'God!' Beth squirmed closer to him for refuge.

'You're not praying,' he teased.

'I—don't have to form words,' she returned. 'He knows everything that's in my mind. I just try to empty out my thoughts to hear His answer.'

'Ah? He answers every prayer?'

'Every one.' She squirmed around again, trying to make out his face. Unable to clearly see, her hand caressed his cheek and traced the form of his lips. 'You don't understand that either, do you, Francis?'

'That God answers every prayer? What a crazy, mixed-up world we'd have if he did.'

'See? I told you so. He *does* answer every one. He really does. But sometimes the answer is *no*!'

'Are you trying to convert me, Ms Beth?'

She giggled. 'That, sir, presupposes that you have some sort of faith to be converted *from*.'

'I knew I should have run when I saw that sign in your eyes.'

'What sign is that?'

'The one that says Baptist.'

'Oh, you awful man!'

'Now *that* I can't let go by,' he threatened. 'It's a man's world, little lady. Don't you forget that. We males are an endangered species. I'm going to have to punish you.'

'Yeah, yeah,' she cheered. 'Punish me like the last time!'

And so another kiss was added to the total. A touching of lips and hearts and bodies until no amount of squirming could bring her as close as she wanted to be. Yet once it was over, Sukey was back in her mind again.

'Do you suppose she *really* hired those boys?'

'When a male gets to be six feet tall I hate to call him a *boy*,' he murmured. 'Thug is more like it. And yes, I'm positive Sue-Ann hired the lot of them.'

'But—but—she's my sister.'

He tilted her chin up and almost touched her nose with his. She could smell and feel the maleness of him, the warm compassion as he gently kissed each of her eyelids. 'You're making a mistake, Beth. You're *her* sister all right, but evidently she's not yours.'

'No! Don't say that!' Fang stirred uneasily at her feet. 'Don't say that,' she repeated in a low, dreary tone, an admission that he might possibly be right. 'But—but where do you suppose she is? She went off in an uproar, and when she loses her temper like that there's no telling——' The telephone ringing interrupted her. She was up in a flash, scattering everything in her lap, almost stepping on Fang, tripping over the radio. But she picked up the telephone receiver just after its second ring. Frank could hear her voice, soft and troubled in the night.

There's only one cure, he told himself. See her through this nightmare, and then marry her. If she'll have me, that is. There have been signs that she cares—a little. If I can only hold on to my temper. Raging at Sue-Ann isn't going to get me anywhere with Beth. Whoever in the world would have thought I'd come down to this little town and find the most wonderful woman in the world? Love and beauty and kindness and affection— and enough sexual response to ride around the world in! I have never *ever* met a woman who turned me on so quickly, so thoroughly, so wonderfully! Man, wait'll I tell Aunt Harriet! He was shaking his head in aston- ishment, and then Beth was back again. Her pale white robe gleamed against the darkness as she hesitated for a moment in the doorway, and then ran across to throw herself at him. His reaction was automatic, gathering her tiny form up in his arms, cuddling her close against his chest, waiting. There were no tears. She seemed to be in a daze; her eyes were wide open, with scarcely a blink.

'Beth?'

She nuzzled against him, and a tiny sob broke from her locked throat.

'Beth?'

'It was the police,' she said in a voice muffled against his shirt. 'They found Sukey's car in a culvert out on the Palestine Road.'

'Well, that's something,' he commented. 'Better than nothing. How is she?'

'They didn't know,' Beth moaned. 'The windshield in front of the driver's seat was cracked, and there was blood on the steering-wheel—but Sukey wasn't there!'

Oh, brother! And what do you say to something like that? he asked himself. The girl was limp in his arms, and still there were no tears. That worried him; there could be no release until there were tears. He shifted one foot and began to propel the swing back and forth. What to say? It sounded a little corny to a man of his sophistication, his worldly veneer, but maybe it would work. He cuddled her closer.

'God will provide,' he whispered.

'Of course,' she said sighing, as if he had recalled something she had temporarily forgotten. And then her body went limp. He tried to move her over into the light from the street lamp. Her face was pale, almost bloodless. Her breath was coming in short, shallow spasms, and her eyes were closed. Sleeping? He shifted her weight again, bringing her legs up on to the swing, cradling her head more comfortably. She stirred not an inch.

'Sleeping,' he muttered to himself. 'You great big idiot, she's fainted!' And so she had; her mind, tortured beyond her strength, had turned itself off. Warily he adjusted her body again, feeling the softness of her thighs, the full roundness of her breasts as they pressed into him, and set himself stoically to guard her through the storm and night.

The telephone rang again at five o'clock in the morning. The clouds were heavier, but somewhere beyond them the sun was at work, and the world could be seen in dull grey. The batteries in his radio had run down—which was just as well. He had heard all he could stand of the fractious hurricane, apparently doing a stately two-step out in the Gulf. Two steps forward, one back, as its internal winds grew higher and higher.

How he managed to get to the phone without awakening the girl in his lap was something he never figured out. But it happened. A tired feminine voice queried him. 'Is Ms Hendley available? This is the emergency-room at Crosby Memorial.'

'She's not available,' he whispered. 'I'm her fiancé, Mr Wylie, the assistant principal at the high school.' It would take all his titles to get them to tell him anything, he was sure. And he was absolutely right. After considerable hemming and hawing an older female voice took over.

'Mr Hendley?'

'Wylie,' he corrected.

'Yes, Mr—er—Wylie. We have just received a patient here in the emergency-room. Her name is—Foster?'

'Sukey!' he yelled. 'Yes. Sue-Ann Foster. My fiancée is her stepsister. What about her?'

'Well, thank the good lord,' the nurse said. 'We weren't sure of her identification. Ms Foster has been in an auto accident. There's some bleeding about the head, but nothing of merit. It would appear, however, that she has a concussion. We have no idea how bad it is. X-rays don't show a skull fracture. In any event, we will admit her to the hospital. Can you—or her step-sister—come to give us the necessary information for our paperwork?'

'Hot damn!' he yelled. 'We'll be there so fast it'll fry your underpants, lady!'

'Well, *really*,' the nurse said sarcastically. She hung up with considerably more enthusiasm than was required.

Crosby Memorial Hospital was barely a handful of blocks away. They pulled into the car park before Beth was fully awake. 'We're here, love,' he coaxed.

'Here? Here where?'

'At the hospital. Don't you remember? I told you that——'

'Oh, lord, yes. Sukey's here! Help me out!' He did, holding her in his arms as he slammed the car door behind them. 'Why—it's raining,' Beth whispered.

'I believe it is.'

'And I'm not dressed, Francis!'

'Neither are three quarters of the people inside this place,' he said, chuckling. 'Hush, now, I've got to get us up these stairs, and you're growing heavier, love.'

Old Dr Tuttle met them at the door. The doctor was tired, his white hair in disarray, and his stethoscope drooped from his coat pocket, almost trailing on the floor. 'Another patient? What's wrong with this one?'

'Not a thing,' Frank replied. 'Sue-Ann Foster was just admitted. We're her relatives.'

'Seen you before.' The old man sighed. 'Ms Beth, of course. Sue-Ann. Little Sukey. Yes, they've just trundled her off to the wards. Concussion, minor cuts and bruises.

Drunk as a skunk, which is probably why she wasn't hurt worse than she was. Mighty lucky young lady. How come you let her go off like that in the storm, Beth?'

'Beth didn't *let* her go off.' Frank felt irritable. As if it were all Beth's fault, for crying out loud. 'Sue-Ann is a grown woman, capable of looking after herself!' Beth tugged at his shirt and whispered.

'Yes,' he agreed. 'Is her condition dangerous?'

'Head's a pretty solid piece of work,' the doctor mused. 'Dangerous? Well, this isn't like spitting watermelon seeds, you know. She's sedated; with her usual luck she'll be all right. Go along with you. I've got a dozen patients already, and if this storm really breaks I suspect there'll be a dozen more! Room twenty-six.'

So they went down the hall in one direction, while the doctor wandered off in the other, still mumbling to himself. 'You can't go in there!' the nurse on station yelled.

'The hell we can't,' Frank returned.

'Don't curse so,' Beth muttered, but hardly stirred out of his arms.

'I'll call a security man,' the nurse threatened.

'Make sure he's a big one!'

'Well, maybe you can go in—just for a minute—if you're her parents.'

'We're her parents.' And with that he pushed through the door and into the two-bed room. The first bed was empty. Sukey Foster was stretched out under the sheet in the second, crowded into the corner up against the windows. Hurricane Ophelia was rattling the frames, spitting huge raindrops down against the glass. But Sukey ignored it all. Flat on her back, arms down at her sides on top of the sheet, with a tiny smile on her face and a big bandage around her head, she lay there.

'Oh, my goodness,' Beth muttered. 'She's dead.'

'She's *not* dead,' Frank assured her. 'Just sleeping.'

'OK,' the nurse said, 'you've had your look. Out. You can wait in the hall.'

'Tough crowd of nurses in this hospital,' Frank muttered.

'You'd better believe it,' the nurse returned. 'Out.'

So he carried Beth out into the hall, and down the corridor a step or two to where a couple of chairs and a wooden bench provided lounging-space. 'I'm going to leave you here while I go stir up a fuss,' he said. As he lowered her gently on to the bench he seemed to groan in relief.

'Heavy?' Beth mumbled.

'Trying to ruin my male ego?' he asked, grinning. 'Of course you're heavy—or maybe I'm just getting weaker.'

'Sorry.'

'Don't worry, I'll get even some day.' He rearranged her robe, settled her down, and laughed again. 'I've lost one of your slippers. We'll have to backtrack it. How long do you want to stay?'

'Until I can talk to Sukey.'

'That could be—a long time.'

'As long as it takes.' With which she slumped over against the carved oak armrest, and her eyes closed.

'As long as it takes,' he whispered. He leaned over her recumbent form, gently brushed the dark curls out of her face, and then kissed the tip of her nose. She smiled at the kiss, a weak, trembling smile, but he was gone, and could not be asked what it all meant.

When next Beth opened her eyes the nurse at the desk was gathering up papers, explaining them to another nurse. And someone was sitting near her on the bench. She wriggled around to look, having trouble focusing.

'Billy Joe? What are you doing here?'

'Them guys told me to wait,' the boy responded. 'The police are comin' sooner or later.'

'The police? We didn't call the police. Not this time.'

Quiet for a moment. The boy's hands were on his knees, palms clutching at his kneecaps. 'He's one big man, that Wylie cat,' he said. 'I thought he was gonna beat my butt—hey, I'm sorry, Ms Beth.'

'I understand,' she said, sighing. With a little effort her hand reached out to land on top of one of his. She offered a comforting pat. 'I thought for a minute he was going to——'

'Kill me dead,' the boy interrupted. 'I thought the same thing. Thought my head was about to fall off. Would have, too, if you hadn't stopped him. Made me think, that did.'

Another silence. Beth looked at him and sighed. All he wanted to do was run. Was that such a great crime? She patted his hand again. 'He's really a very nice man.'

Another silence.

'Ms Beth, do you really believe all that stuff you keep pushin' at me?'

'About studying, and like that? Yes, I really believe in it, Billy Joe.'

'And him? Does he believe it? I looked him up down at the *Item*. Lord, he was a holy terror when he played for the Falcons. They say he used to tear players apart, but now—he's just a nice guy. Nice guys finish last.'

'Depends on how nice,' she offered glumly.

'And he got that doctor's thing from football?'

'Well, not quite, Billy Joe. He got that doctor's thing *after* he played football. Nobody can play forever. Even Joe Namath had to stop some time.'

'S'pose you're right,' the boy muttered. Finally, for the first time, his head turned in her direction. 'You're nice too, Ms Beth,' he said. 'An' you're a lot tougher than *he* is.'

'Do you say so?' She chuckled as she struggled to keep her eyes open. This was undoubtedly one of the strangest conversations she had ever had with a student. How do you suppose Frank would react to a statement like that? she asked herself. He and I will have to talk—and in that moment Frank's image was replaced by Sukey, lying there in the bed, as close to death as could be, and all because of Frank.

'Oh, dear lord,' she muttered. Sukey and Frank. I want Frank, Sukey wants Frank, and heaven only knows who or what Frank wants! And if Sukey can't have him she'll go off in her car again almost any time soon, and really kill herself! So what do I do? Fight her off? Or give way to her the way I've done for all these years? After all, Sue-Ann can't help it if she was born a little— hypersensitive; she *is* my sister, and I did promise Mama!

Beth didn't want an answer, either from herself or from Frank. She just wanted to sit there on that hard wooden bench and cry herself away until nothing was left but one slipper and a pool of tears. But that was something she *couldn't* do. Her Baptist conscience, her sense of duty, would not allow it. So she brushed the incipient tears away, and turned back to the boy.

'Well, just what are you waiting for, Billy Joe?'

The tired eyes in the thin face looked at her slowly. 'Do you really care what happens to me?' he asked. His counter-question disturbed her. 'Really *me*, not just one of a bunch of guys?'

'Of course I care.'

'And him? Mr Wylie. Does *he* care about me?' Beth Hendley took a deep breath and took a good look at the tall, thin young man beside her. Locked inside that gangly frame there was a real person calling to her for help. She could hear it clearly. Her answer must be cautious.

'Yes. Mr Wylie cares. He's a very caring man.'

'Do you s'pose I'm too late to change?'

'Never. Nobody is ever too late to change.'

'All I ever wanted to do was run.' He sighed. 'But . . .'

'All you need is help, Billy Joe. We'll help you, Mr Wylie and I. It won't be easy, but maybe if you work hard enough at it you can still run!'

He gave an audible sigh and slumped down into normal teenage posture, abandoning that stiff pride that had sustained him. 'A positive maybe?' he asked. She nodded her head and grinned. 'Well, what d'ya know,' he commented as he grinned. 'I'm waiting for the police to come, Ms Beth. They want me to give a statement about your sister.'

And now the shoe was on the other foot. 'My sister?' she asked tentatively.

'That blonde lady. Sukey, the doctor called her. Your sister?'

'My sister,' she agreed, crossing her fingers behind her back.

And then he threw her another curve. 'She got all her marbles, that lady?'

'I—er—believe she does, Billy Joe. Not arranged like yours and mine, but—you know, it takes different strokes for different folks. What happened?'

'I don't rightly know,' Billy Joe said. 'She said she wanted to meet us all after that—after what we did at your house, you know. Over by the gate of the Arboretum. But I got there late, and a couple of the guys says she was there and all, but then she floored her go-pedal and went roaring down the Palestine Road. That ain't no road for a woman to go speeding down, not in no storm like this. So I followed her. I almost

caught up to her, but she was maybe a quarter of a mile
ahead of me when she hit that cement culvert, and the
wind it just throwed her off the road, you know.'

'Oh, Billy Joe! And you got help?'

'Couldn't find no help,' he said. 'Anybody with sense
in their heads was home. I was pretty scared. In all them
movies, the gas tank busts and the car blows up, ya know.
So I managed to pull her out the front window and
carried her back to my car. Thought she was dead, I did,
but how can ya tell? I stuffs her in the front seat, and
brought her back here to the hospital. And that car never
did blow up. Sometimes I think them TV shows are a
bunch of bull——'

'Maybe they are.' Beth laughed as she cut him off.
'Oh, Billy Joe, what a brave thing to do!' She managed
to struggle to her feet, and he rose too. The tile floor
was cold under her non-slippered foot, but she hugged
him with a great deal of enthusiasm, and laughed as his
face turned red. Stretching up on tiptoes she managed
a kiss that missed his dodging mouth and landed on his
nose.

'Didn't you ever kiss a girl before, Billy Joe?' she
teased.

'Not no old broad,' he muttered. 'I mean——'

'I know what you mean.' She chuckled, and then
turned serious. 'You probably saved my sister's life, Billy
Joe. I shall be forever grateful to you for that.' The boy
blushed even deeper, until his cheeks matched the colour
of his hair. And that was the way that Frank found them.

'And what, do I suppose, is going on here?' Frank
was putting on an act, but the boy took him seriously.

'Hey, I didn't have nothin' to do with it,' he muttered
nervously. He detached Beth's arms and managed a step
away from her. 'I wouldn't have—well, you *said* she was
your woman, and—and she upped and wrapped herself

around me like Saran wrap, and then I'm da—darned—
if she didn't kiss me to boot!'

'Yes. Does that a lot, she does,' Frank Wylie agreed.
'Always enjoyed it, myself. You didn't?'

'I was too scared to,' Billy Joe admitted. 'I remember
what you said about grinding my bones—hey, I don't
know. I don't get to kiss many old—many school-
teachers.'

Beth moved over to Frank's side and leaned against
him. His arm automatically came around her shoulders.
'Old broad is what he called me,' she said firmly. 'Old
broad!'

'You *are* getting on,' Frank teased, and then laughed
at her. She had stamped on his foot with her slipper,
and felt the pain more than he did.

'In case you don't know,' she continued, 'Billy Joe is
the one who found Sukey. He pulled her out of her car
and brought her over here.'

'I know.'

She made a little face at him. 'You think that you
know everything,' she accused him.

'Men are naturally superior,' he agreed. She wished
mightily that she might be wearing her pumps with the
three-inch stiletto heels, but it was all to no avail.

'Do you s'pose they're gonna arrest me?' Billy Joe
asked cautiously.

'Arrest you? For what, Billy Joe? You're a hero!'

'You gotta be kiddin'. Even my mother wouldn't believe that, and she's willin' to believe almost anything.'

'Then you wait until the next issue of the *Picayune
Item*,' Frank assured him. 'There's a reporter on the way
over now. Big headlines, I'll bet—Picayune Man Saves
Life.'

'Man? They gonna call me a man?'

'Well, I suppose they might want to say "youth", but "man" sounds more like it, doesn't it? I'll use my influence.'

'Ain't no reporter gonna come out in this storm to interview Billy Joe,' the boy grumbled. 'Gotta be crazy to do that.'

'That's what it takes to be a reporter,' Frank assured him. 'She's crazy. And good-looking, too. And when I talked to her last she and the duty sergeant at the police headquarters were getting into the car to come. After all, it's not very far.'

'I don't believe they'll come,' Billy Joe insisted. But they came anyway. And when they were done, and Billy Joe went home triumphantly in a police car—with the lights and siren working, as he'd requested—Frank looked around at Beth and said, 'Come on, little love. Sukey won't be awake for hours yet. Let's get you dressed.'

Which sent a shiver of excitement up and down Beth's spine, because while the words were innocuous, even the most naïve of girls could tell by the look in his eye that he meant 'undressed'. And she wasn't at all sure how to respond. Not yet, at least.

Sukey awoke at noon. Picayune was in the midst of that deadly calm before a hurricane really arrived. The streets were practically empty. Most citizens had done their emergency shopping. The schools were closed. Merchants had boarded up their front windows. The world was merely waiting. And Sukey Foster opened those big blue eyes of hers and smiled.

'Beth? What are you doing here?'

'Waiting for you, silly. How do you feel?'

One of the patient's hands went to her head. 'They cut my hair? Don't tell me they cut my hair!' All said in a wail of alarm.

'It'll all grow back soon enough.' There, that was what big sisters said in times like these, wasn't it? 'How do you feel?'

'I—have a little headache. Oh, Beth, I feel like a fool— such a fool. I lost my temper, and——' And the tears interrupted. The doctor had left instructions. Keep her calm and quiet. 'What have I done to you?' the patient moaned.

Beth climbed stiffly out of her chair. She had been sitting by the bedside since early in the morning, and none of her limbs wanted to respond. She leaned over the bed and gently hugged her stepsister. 'You haven't done *anything* to me, love,' she said softly. 'Everything's all right. You would be too if it weren't for that damn hurricane out there in the Gulf, waiting to pounce on us!'

But Sukey would have none of that. A tear slipped down her almost perfect cheek. 'And Frank,' she cried. 'Poor, wonderful Frank.'

Yes, poor, wonderful Frank, Beth thought as she sank back into her chair, her head going around in circles. Poor, wonderful Frank who had, just a few hours earlier, over a cup of the worst coffee she had ever drunk in her life, asked her to marry him. Poor, wonderful Frank.

And she, poor, not-so-wonderful Beth Hendley, had looked thoughtfully up at him, her heart pounding thirteen to the dozen, and said she loved him—but would have to talk to Sukey first.

'You never talked like that before,' the patient said, interrupting her thoughts.

'Oh? Like what?'

'You said *damn* hurricane, Beth. You never talked like that before.'

'No, I guess I never did, love. Some things have changed. You gave us quite a scare, you know.'

'Did I?' Sukey preened herself, as if proud that she had become the centre of attraction. 'I didn't get to New Orleans. I found this place down in Slidell.' And then, 'When is Frank coming to see me?'

'As soon as you're well enough. Since he's not a relative, the hospital people would prefer—well, they worry about you, dear. No excitement.'

'Yes, of course. And if Frank came, there'd be excitement, wouldn't there? Did you know——?'

Whatever it was Beth might not know just didn't make it to the starting-gate. Old Dr Tuttle shambled into the room, followed by a tall, handsome newcomer, who smiled a lot. 'I'm gonna go home to bed for a month,' the older man said. 'Make you known to Dr Porterman, the newest member of our staff. Your Mr Wylie suggested the patient might respond better with a younger doctor.'

'You may call me Michael,' the new doctor said as he moved to the side of the bed and reached for Sukey's wrist. One hardly needed to be a specialist to note the flash of interest that sparked out of those big blue eyes. And the frank appraisal returned by Michael Porterman.

'Frank sent you?' Sukey's cheeks flushed.

'Asked me to come,' the doctor corrected as he bent over to flash his little penlight into her eyes. 'Hmmm. Not bad at all, considering your wild adventures, young lady. Now, get some sleep. I'll be along later to give you a—more thorough examination.'

'Yes,' Sukey murmured. 'Oh, Beth!' She lay back on her pillow with both eyes closed.

Is it possible? Beth asked herself.

'Wasn't that wonderful of Frank to go to all that trouble?' her stepsister asked. 'I hope he comes soon.'

No, it's not possible. She's fixated, Beth thought. There's no hope.

'He'll be along soon,' she coaxed. 'Now, close your eyes again, and get some rest.'

'Beth—you won't ever leave me, will you? You promised Mama——'

'I remember, love. No, I won't leave you. I'll be beside you for as long as you want me.' And you won't ever leave me, will you, Sukey? One of us is wearing an albatross around her neck. Or maybe both of us are? She ducked her head to hide her own tears. So many promises, so much responsibility. And earlier this morning she had almost felt the weight of it shift on to broader shoulders than hers. Almost the burden had gone. Almost.

Frank Wylie chose that moment to come into the room. Or maybe it was fate that did the choosing. He walked over to the bed quietly and stood by Beth's chair, picking up her hand to cherish as he leaned over the bed. 'Asleep?'

'Yes,' Beth whispered. 'Just now. She asked for you.'

'Did she really? I wonder why.'

'Frank, maybe we could go out in the hall?'

He looked down at her gravely. 'I don't like the sound of that, Beth. You've come to a decision?' She nodded. His gentle hand pulled her to her feet and half supported her to the door and outside. She turned for a second to look back at the recumbent figure in the bed. Sukey was smiling again.

'Well, her dreams are pleasant,' she muttered as she tucked her hand under Frank's elbow. 'Do you suppose we could go outside?'

'Probably.' He led her down the corridor to the main door, and pushed it open. The wind was sighing, a mourning sound, the sort of noise a witch might make while stirring her cauldron. 'Maybe we can make a few minutes. The air smells clean, doesn't it?'

'It does.' Clean and clear, and she could hardly contain herself as she clung to him, using both hands. All those plans, all those wild dreams, all that yearning. There were tears in her eyes, brought on by the wind, of course. Or at least she told herself that. As for Frank, he spread his legs slightly to maintain a balance against the force of the storm, and stared down at her, his face like a rock construction, as if he knew already what she had to say. Which made it all that much harder to say at all.

'Oh, Francis,' she said quietly.

'Can't say it? Is it that bad?'

'Yes, my dear. I—can't marry you.'

His free hand came around her, pressing her relentlessly into his chest. 'Can't or won't?'

'Does it matter?'

'No, I suppose it doesn't. May I know why?'

'I—I know it sounds silly, but—it's Sukey.'

'Sue-Ann? How does she figure in between you and I, Beth?'

'She—wants you, Frank.'

'And because she wants me, you won't have me?'

'I—please, Frank, don't make it any harder on me. It's about all I can bear at the moment.'

'But that's the truth, isn't it? You didn't talk like this earlier this morning, over at your house.'

'But—but I didn't know then what Sukey felt. I thought that——'

'Promises?'

'I promised my mother I'd look after her. Maybe it's only a habit—maybe it's a duty. I don't know. I'm so mixed up. I can't seem to think straight.' The wind rose a notch, and a splatter of rain touched them.

'We could be—friends, Francis?' She could not know it, but she used his name like a caress. 'We could see each other from time to time?'

He frowned down at her. 'Friends? I don't think so, Beth. In fact, I suppose I'll be winding up my work in Picayune sooner than I had planned.'

It was like a blow to the heart. She swallowed hard. 'You'll find someone else,' she whispered, all the while praying that it might never be so. I want him to be happy, the proud side of her said. Not without me, the other side of her conscience returned. Not without me.

'You're sure, Beth?'

'I *have* to be sure,' she responded. Her lips were forming words, but her throat would not let them pass. And the tears.

'Then I guess there's nothing more to be said,' Frank Wylie told her as he gently untangled her arm, looked at her with his heart in his eyes, and then turned and walked briskly down to the pavement.

'Oh, God,' Beth muttered as she watched his tall figure cross the boulevard. 'Oh, God, what have I done?' The wind rose another notch; rain pelted at her, and if God answered, Beth Hendley did not receive the message.

CHAPTER TEN

FOR twenty minutes or more Beth Hendley stood just outside the hospital door like a statue, being pelted with more and more rain as the storm's volume increased. Frank was gone. He hadn't turned to wave when he'd reached his car, merely climbed in, started the motor, and swept off down the street. Only twenty minutes, and already the hole in her heart had grown as large as Mammoth Cave. An empty cave, where words echoed off odd corners and came back to haunt her. I love you, Francis! It tore at her mind.

There was something to be said for the strong, stable sort of woman that Beth Hendley had always been. But when she finally broke down she fell into tiny little pieces, little whirling lights and shadows, full of fears and tears and remorse. Her body finally stumbled back into the shelter of the hospital; her mind could find no such shelter. She wandered down the hall, a vacant look on her face.

'Ms Hendley?' The nurse on station took one look at that face and came around her desk. 'Can I help you?'

'No.' Said gruffly, flatly, accompanied by a little push. The nurse backed off, while Beth went down to Sukey's room and pushed the door open. The dying patient had made a miraculous recovery. Sue-Ann was smiling happily up into the eyes of Dr Michael Porterman, who was breaking that most sacred hospital rule, and was sitting on her bed. Sukey's high-pitched giggle indicated no sign of cranial damage. And the doctor seemed to be enjoying himself as well.

'Why, Beth, you're soaking wet,' the invalid said.

'I was outside saying goodbye to Frank Wylie,' Beth replied as she walked over to the bed. The doctor removed himself as if he had been caught committing one of the cardinal sins.

'Well.' Sukey pouted. 'I'm glad he's gone. He's such a bore. So serious and all.'

'You're *glad* he's *gone*?' It took all Beth's tiny residue of self-control to keep from shouting. 'You're *glad*——'

'Yes,' her stepsister admitted. 'Glad he's gone. He was only interested in my money, and he's far too old for me.' And then archly, 'You should have made a play for him yourself, Beth. He's just your type.'

'Play for him? Type?' The words wandered out vaguely. Beth Hendley was standing by the side of the bed, but nobody was at the controls inside her mind.

'But then of course you don't have any money,' Sukey concluded sadly.

'Don't have any money?' Beth stared down at the patient, working hard to construct some order to things. 'You—you don't love Frank?'

'Of course I don't, silly. He's so—foreboding! What a silly idea!' And again that giggle and the long eye-lashes flashing in Michael Porterman's direction.

What a silly idea, Beth thought. It was a thought to grab on to. What a silly idea. Why did I give Frank up for this flaming little idiot? My sister?

'No, she's not really my sister,' Sukey was saying to the doctor. 'Stepsister, yes. But really, we're no relation at all, you know. We don't look alike, and we don't think alike...'

And I'll kill the little monster, Beth told herself. The rage didn't have to be summoned. It came of itself, boiling down through her empty mind like water returning to a blocked stream.

'I think we'd better go,' the doctor said, breaking in on her train of thought just in time.

'Yes,' Beth muttered. 'You're *not* my sister, are you, Sukey?' She turned away woodenly, and struggled towards the door. Dr Porterman was right behind her, chattering to Sukey until the door closed behind them.

'A sparkling lady,' the doctor told Beth. 'Full of life.'

'Yes, and all that lovely money,' Beth mused. The doctor blushed, and turned away. Beth continued to wander down the hall in the general direction of the front door.

There was nobody on the streets except for herself. Beth wandered in the general direction of home, still thoroughly confused. Hurricane Ophelia had finally decided to move ashore, but not where expected. She rumbled and mumbled and swung west, heading for the Texas panhandle. And as she turned, her frisky tail sent one provocative strike in Picayune's direction. The trees along Goodyear Boulevard were bending before the storm. Bending and swaying, and occasionally cracking as a bough broke and went whirling down the wind.

'Somebody could get hurt,' Beth told herself, but it wasn't a thought that was related to *her*. Just that amorphous *somebody*. And since God looked after fools and madwomen, she arrived in front of her own house without a scratch.

A loose shutter was banging from the back of the house, and Fang, who had been confined alone in the house during all this, was barking feebly in the distance. The garage door was partially ajar, and she could see that her car was soaked. It didn't seem to matter. She folded her arms across her chest and looked. Her soaked hair had finally lost its curls, and was hanging down over her face like the end of an old mop. She brushed it aside, but it returned in a moment. And someone else, leaning over her shoulders, brushed it away for her.

'Only an idiot would stand out here in the rain!' Frank Wylie shouted from behind her.

For some reason Beth was not surprised. Frank *ought* to have been there, and therefore he was. She leaned back against his soaked chest. 'And only an idiot would stand with her and criticise!' she yelled. Anger and tears and storm all mixed together. 'Look at that!' she yelled, gesturing towards her house. 'I don't have a sister!' Her mind was still whirling about in little circles, going nowhere.

'Do you say so?'

'And I don't have any money!'

'Ah. That's important?'

'All I own in the world are my dog and my house, and, dear lord, how am I going to spend the rest of my life with *them*? Am I going to be a spinster schoolteacher?'

That was the moment that Fang managed to break loose from the house. The little dog came hurtling down the front stairs, yapping, and ended up hiding behind a capacious leg—Frank's leg.

'For pity's sake!' Beth screamed, 'I don't even have a dog! You've stolen my dog, damn you! Now all I have in the whole wide world is a house!'

If ever there was a time of judgement, this was it. It seemed to be the God of Abraham that answered. Thunder rolled in the winds. Between the garage and the house stood the stately old oak tree. Planted on that Easter Sunday of 1865 as a memorial, just a week after General Lee had gone down to the little court-house at Appomattox to meet with General Grant, it had long since lost its core to rot and insects. And now Ophelia pushed, the tree resisted, the thunder rolled, wind and tree struggled, and gently, ever so gently, the oak tree rocked, twisted, and fell down, squarely across the roof of Beth Hendley's house. For another second the house seemed to resist, and then it too, not the youngest building in Picayune, crumpled in the middle and collapsed.

'And now you don't seem to have a house.' The words were calmly spoken, at her ear, and his arms were around her.

'And now I don't have a house.' The idea hadn't permeated yet. Her mind fumbled for an answer. Everything she owned was gone: sister Sukey, her dog, her house. And probably my job as well, she thought. 'And now I don't have a house,' she repeated as she leaned back against him. 'Or anything else. Just Beth Hendley— nothing else.'

'Not *exactly* correct,' he told her, and then chuckled.

A tiny spark flared for a moment. Anger conquered many ills. She groped in her mind and found a thread of sense remaining. 'You needn't laugh at me,' she snapped. 'I don't have *anything* left. That's not funny!'

He turned her around and wiped the water off her face. 'Of course it's not funny,' he said. 'I think it's all bad luck. What you need to do is change your name. How can you be lucky with a name like Hendley?'

'Frank, I'm too stupid for word games,' she cried. 'Spell it out.'

'You still have me,' he said solemnly.

'I—still have you?' She brushed her hair back and stared up at him. He was as wet as she, as wet and—as serious? 'I still have you, Francis?'

'All you have to do is reach out and take, Beth. And I still have a house and a job and——'

A wild thought crossed her mind. 'Frank? How come Dr Porterman suddenly took over Sukey—er—Sukey's case?'

'Good-looking man,' he averred. 'We went to school together. Old friends. We've done a lot of favours for each other over the years. Go for him, did she?'

'You *knew* she would, Frank Wylie! Lord, are there no limits to what you'll do?'

'None at all,' he admitted brazenly. 'None at all. Well?'

There was a flash of noise at their feet, a final creaking as the ancient oak settled. A last squeal as nails pulled loose in the old, totally ruined house.

'Beth?'

Somehow she was up in his arms again, held tightly against his chest. Somehow the excitement inside her seemed stronger than that outside. Her mind wandered. 'I've got to get out of these wet things.'

'I have some thoughts along those lines.' He jiggled her a little to redistribute her weight. 'But I don't intend to carry you around like this forever, Beth.'

'Just reach out and take?'

'That's the idea,' he returned.

Well, Beth Hendley, she told herself in her best lecture tone, why should *you* be the last one on the block to know what's going on? And she reached out her hands around his strong neck, and took.

**THIS JULY, HARLEQUIN OFFERS YOU
THE PERFECT SUMMER READ!**

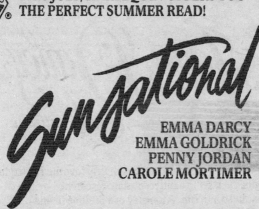

Sunsational

**EMMA DARCY
EMMA GOLDRICK
PENNY JORDAN
CAROLE MORTIMER**

From top authors of Harlequin Presents comes
HARLEQUIN SUNSATIONAL, a four-stories-in-one
book with 768 pages of romantic reading.

Written by such prolific Harlequin authors as Emma Darcy,
Emma Goldrick, Penny Jordan and Carole Mortimer,
HARLEQUIN SUNSATIONAL is the perfect summer
companion to take along to the beach, cottage, on your
dream destination or just for reading at home in the warm
sunshine!

Don't miss this unique reading opportunity.

Available wherever Harlequin books are sold.

SUN

Back by Popular Demand

Janet Dailey

Americana

A romantic tour of America through fifty favorite Harlequin Presents, each set in a different state researched by Janet and her husband, Bill. A journey of a lifetime in one cherished collection.

In August, don't miss the exciting states featured in:

Title #13 — ILLINOIS
      The Lyon's Share

   #14 — INDIANA
      The Indy Man

Available wherever Harlequin books are sold.

JD-AUG